Absurd Delights

A HunterxVampire Romance

Monroe Wildrose

Teapots and Stolen Souls Publishing

The First Edition was published in 2024 by Teapots and Stolen Souls Publishing.

Cover Design by @zzukaritass

Contents

Titles by Monroe Wildrose

Seas of Marecult Duology
Fortune of Emerald and Salt
Fate of Ruby and Throne

Tales of Farivein
Clementine's Parlor of the Extraordinary and Curious
Tailor Troubles

Booker Brothers Duet
Too Sweet
Absurd Delights

Published Anthologies
Femme Fairytales
A Grimoire of Honeyed Spells

Last we saw the Booker Brothers:

In **Too Sweet**, Briar, a human girl with boyfriend trouble, told her ex, Morgan (vampire hunter), that she is dating Darcy Booker (vampire). Unaware that vampires or hunters exist, Briar asks Darcy to fake date her to make Morgan jealous.

Briar starts hanging out with the gang (Darcy, Crispin, Maisie, Trudy, and Erik), and fake feelings turn very real as Briar and Darcy start to fall for each other. A series of mishaps happen, such as Darcy accidentally biting Briar, Briar finding out about Darcy's vampirism, and Morgan becoming increasingly fixated with breaking them up.

Eventually, Morgan, his dad, and his brother, all vampire hunters, kidnap Briar to entrap Darcy and Crispin. Maisie offers to help the Booker brothers on their rescue mission, even though she is a vampire hunter.

At the end of **Too Sweet**, we learn that Maisie and Crispin have been recruited by The Order of Vampires Affiliation and The Hunters Guild to get married and become a public face for peace between the two factions.

Character Glossary

Maisie Pope: A teenage vampire hunter, from a wealthy family of hunters. Went to high school with Crispin and Darcy.

Crispin Booker: A teenage vampire, biological mom was from an affluent vampire family. Both biological parents died, and he was adopted by The Bookers.

Darcy Booker: Crispin's adopted younger brother. Also a vampire, with a human Girlfriend, Briar. Sunshine/Cinnamon Roll boy.

Briar Grey: Darcy's girlfriend, a human with type 1 diabetes and a bad attitude.

Trudy: Maisie's best friend. Does not know about Vampires and hunters. Dating Erik.

Erik: Crispin and Darcy's friend from High School. Does not know about vampires or hunters. Dating Trudy.

Kat Booker: Crispin's adopted mom and vampire. Was best friends with Crispin's biological mom, Liza.

Nolan Booker: Crispin's adopted dad, and vampire.

Helena Pope: Maisie's mom, a vampire hunter.

William Pope: Maisie's dad, a vampire hunter.

Kirk Hillbrand: Crispin's maternal grandfather, an old money vampire.

Jaggar Hillbrand: Crispin's cousin, vampire.

Fern: Jaggar's girlfriend, vampire.

Ajay Harrison: Maisie's Ex-Boyfriend, vampire hunter.

Morgan Pope: Maisie's Cousin, Briar's Ex-Boyfriend, vampire hunter.

Jessica: Maisie and Crispin's handler, vampire hunter, works for The Hunter's Guild.

Liza Hillbrand-Farrow: Crispin's biological mother, vampire. Kat Booker's best friend.

Matthew Farrow: Crispin's biological father, vampire.

The Haymaks: Old money vampire hunter family

The Steeles: Political vampire couple.

Content Warnings

Following are some subjects that are touched on that I would like you to be aware of before reading this story:

Violence
Blood
Anxiety representation (including on-page anxiety attacks)
Adoption (Character processes some thoughts on being adopted)
Sexual harassment
Underage drinking
Underage use of tobacco products
Sexual Situation and off page intimacy
Biting
Language
Drugging

To all my anxiety girls who get told, "don't be anxious."
Don't punch those people, besties; an open-palm slap is more dramatic.

One

Crispin

"I'm not sure boba and blood is a great combo." I stood in my wedding suit with a straw stuck into a drink my brother made me. The thick blood ran up the tube, and the boba bubbles came up with it.

Some days I wished I sucked blood straight from the vein of a live person. Not that I ever had, but they said something was calming about it, like a drug hitting your system. Cold blood bags didn't have the same effect. They were nourishment, not pleasure.

Maybe I should have taken up smoking, like my soon-to-be wife.

Wife.

"Yeah, it's a little weird, I agree." Darcy was looking at the boba in the bottom of his glass, licking away a drop of blood at the corner of his mouth.

"It's like that time you tried to make us blood milkshakes."

"Also, not my greatest idea, but we did learn that blood and milk-based products are a no-go." He smiled at me, lifting his straw to avoid the pearls but sucked almost all the blood down.

I did the same, leaving crimson-soaked leftovers at the glass's bottom.

"Maybe we should just drink it from blood bags instead of trying to be creative." I sat next to him on the groom's suite couch.

The Pope's had fresh blood delivered to the suite like a weird wedding gift. Something about a prestigious family of hunters delivering blood to vampires felt wrong. The Order of Vampire Affiliation, or OOVA for short, had paid for this entire shindig and paid for everyone to drive two hours away. They paid for this ritzy hotel and the garden in the back where we would have a quaint five-hundred-person ceremony and then the grand ballroom, packed to the brim with high-ranking vampires and hunters alike.

What an absolute nightmare.

"You alright?" Darcy asked, mouth quirking into an awkward smile.

"Fuck no." I gave him a skeptical look, and he reached back to rub the back of his neck.

"Yeah, that makes sense. Sorry I asked."

I felt slightly sour and said, "I'm glad you're here as my best man. I don't even know...what's his name...Jiminy Cricket..."

"Jaggar. You know his name is Jaggar."

My cousin on my mother's side. I had only met him two days ago, and what a trip that had been. He looked so much like me. His blond hair was much longer and curly, but we had the same blue eyes and sharp features. His vibe was more surfer with a rolled beanie, but it still gave me a weird feeling in my chest. Jagger Hillbrand and all my other dickwad family.

I was the bastard vampire prince of them all.

That's what Darcy called me, at least. My mother, Liza, had been as close to a vampire princess as you could get in the order. That was before she met my dad and changed her name to Liza Farrow. My dad and mom had been happy, at least that's what Mom and Dad said.

What a fucked up sentence.

There was a knock on the door then, and my mother and father crept in, ensuring we were decent. My mother looked beautiful in a black beaded gown, and my father had a crisp tuxedo on with his hair slicked back. I smiled, glimpsing a picture of them when they were younger and newly in love.

The wedding was pink and black. All the guests were allowed to wear grey, white, and black attire. My tuxedo was classic white and black, but Darcy's was black on black, just as Erik's and Jagger's were.

Mom's eyes welled up with tears as she saw us—My adopted parents, Nolan and Kat Booker. The people who had always cared for me, treated me as their own. They had given me every opportunity they could afford, even though I wasn't their blood. They were good people, and I would do anything for them.

Hence the marriage.

"My boys, I cannot believe how handsome you look," my mom choked out, dabbing at her tears with a handkerchief my dad handed her.

"You look awesome, Mom," Darcy said, springing up to wrap her in a hug.

"Oh, psh, this old thing?"

"That old thing is actually very new," my dad said under his breath, and I smiled.

I walked to a cooler that held my mom's corsage—an explosion of pink blooms and greenery. Maisie had ordered it for her, and I was grateful, though I hadn't told her that.

"This is for you, Mom," I said, walking back over to her and slipping the small bouquet on her wrist.

She let me put it on before my dad came and stood beside her. They had their 'we need to talk about something serious' faces, and I braced myself for impact.

"Crispin, you don't have to do this." My dad started. The same things they had been telling me for three months. Now that summer had come and gone, I had heard these lines almost daily.

Only today was the last day they could say it. It was their last day to try to talk reason into me. I don't think they understood. They only knew that OOVA and The Hunter's Guild pitched us the idea. They didn't know that they had privately offered Maisie and me whatever our hearts desired that was within their power to grant. With two of the most influential organizations in the world, there wasn't much they couldn't do.

So, while my parents may not know everything, and Maisie and my decision to do this may seem crazy, it was worth it.

My parents' house and cars would be paid off. Their retirement would be wholly paid for, and very well at that. Briar Grey would never have to worry about diabetes supplies again in her life. Even if she broke up with Darcy, The Order assured me her health needs would be met.

For five years of marriage to a girl that drove me crazy, it seemed worth it. A few appearances at some balls, birthdays, and uppity vampire houses. It was worth it.

I had no idea what Maisie had asked for, and I didn't care much.

"We will support you no matter what. Even if you want to walk out of this hotel room and go home." My mom touched my shoulder to ensure I was paying attention.

"Will you support me standing under that garden arch downstairs?" I asked, willing my mom not to cry another tear. She only smiled, squeezing one shoulder.

"Of course we will, Crispin," Dad said, pulling me into him as we hugged cheesily in the hotel room.

I was going to throw up. Where did one throw up during a pink garden ceremony? I clenched my hands together, sweating profusely despite the mild September weather.

"It'll be alright," Darcy whispered to me.

I tried to breathe more regularly. Trudy and Darcy had come down the aisle. Then Erik and Briar, and finally Jaggar and Maisie's cousin Mila.

The seconds between that and when Maisie was supposed to come out were agonizingly slow. But then the music came—*the* music, and everyone rose and turned, and I stood stock still.

Maisie was hot. I'd always thought so—Irritating and belligerent but hot. However, as she walked down the aisle, hot was the last word that fit.

She was ethereal, divine even, in her blush pink satin dress and veil.

She looked up at me, and the knot in my stomach turned to raging nausea once more.

She deserved better than this. She deserved better than me.

She deserved a man who would weep at the sight of her walking toward him, like in the movies. I remember the video of my dad crying like a baby when my mom walked to him.

The pink flowers left their lingering scent as time slowed, and the breeze shifted her veil. She looked like she belonged here. While I was out of place among the ornate fixtures and expensive napkins, the Princess of Riverside was as perfect as ever. Living her cotton candy spoiled rich kid life.

"Who gives this woman to be married?" the minister asks.

Woman, she's nineteen years old. She's a child. Hell, we are both fucking children.

I should have yelled it out, screamed it, to all the rich people who came to see the spectacle. But it wasn't just me in this now. I wouldn't ruin her chance to get whatever she wanted, and I wouldn't cheat my loved ones out of something I could obtain for them. So I kept quiet as Maisie's father came forward, his face cold and distant as he announced himself, and I stepped forward to take his daughter's hand.

"Don't trip me, Moron," she whispered so that only I could hear it.

"Take it easy, Princess. It's the happiest day of our lives."

Two

Maisie

I needed a cigarette.

I tried to control my breathing on the floor of the bathroom. The pressure in my chest was lifting now, the weight of it not so crushing as it had been. My hands were still trembling, though I had them fisted in my lap.

Breathe. Breathe. Breathe.

I tried to remember the breathing exercises that Dr. Handa taught me. I looked at the open pill bottle on the counter. Thirty minutes ago, I opened it like the contents were my lifeline. I felt relieved when I looked at the medication spilled from the shaky open. I still held the single pill in my hand that I had intended to take, but talked myself out of.

Even if it was my prescription, I tried to play a game. How long can the spoiled rich girl go without taking the Xanax her therapist prescribed? Every time, I swore I wouldn't take another. They made me feel distant, like I was seeing everything through a window underwater.

This might be the only wedding I ever had, and I didn't want to feel like I was fighting to walk down the aisle. Even if it was a sham, and even if Crispin irritated the ever-living shit out of me.

I swept myself up, taking a few more deep breaths as I shoveled the pills back into the bottle and sealed the safety cap. I threw them into the open bag on the back of the toilet. I braced my arms on the hotel bathroom counter, looking at the dark circles under my eyes. Wasn't I too young for those? Oh well, nothing a little color correction concealer couldn't fix.

I heard a knock at the hotel room door, and a gaggle of voices came through.

It was show time.

You may now kiss the bride had never been less romantic, I was sure of it.

The pressure of Cripin's pursed mouth over mine was filled with emotion, but those emotions were resentment, anger, and disgust. He pulled back and smiled out at the crowd, who clapped politely. I caught sight of Darcy wincing a bit as the bridal party left the stage.

We took very staged photos, and I was sure that every single one returned from the overpriced photographer would reveal the truth. No matter what position she put us in or the hand placement, Crispin Booker and I weren't in love.

Which would be fine, except we weren't just required to be married. We were supposed to make everyone believe we were in love, and it was proving much more complex than I had initially thought.

I stood at the bar waiting for my cranberry tonic, glaring at my husband, who was dancing, smiling, and joking with Erik. He seemed so unbothered by everything it made me sick, like this meant nothing to him. His easy smiles and frequent eye rolls made his feelings about The Order and The Guild very clear.

It had been surprising to find out that Crispin was a Hillbrand. They were one of the most influential vampire families, with old money and even older ties and connections. However, the way they all acted cold and distant from Crispin, more distant than these families acted normally, had me intrigued by their story. I knew he was adopted, and Nolan and Kat were some of the nicest people I had ever met. Not fake nice, either. I could tell they loved Crispin with the sort of love I had always wanted to feel from my parents. As if to prove my point, I watched as Kat Booker came and threw her arms around Crispin, dabbing her eyes with a handkerchief. It made me look at my own father, who was talking with some of his friends, gesturing to the grandness of the sparkling ballroom before him, as if he had paid for it himself.

"Hey there, Pope." A heady and smooth voice came to me that I recognized immediately.

"Ajay," I tuned, smiling, my cheeks turning pink. "And It's Pope-Booker, now."

He looked handsome, but then again, he always did. His dark brown hair swept away from his face to reveal molten brown eyes.

His suit fit perfectly, and the smell of amber and a heavier spice wafted off of him. The hard thing about Ajay was that he was aware of how he looked, and how much money his family had. But damn, was he charming. There was a reason I had fallen hard for him in my junior year when he had just gone off to college. Our parents had dinner together often enough that we had no trouble starting a fling. I even lost my virginity in the back of his Mercedes. He wined and dined me almost as well as he had my parents. My mother had been fawning over him, so sure, he was the one for me. However, we lost touch during my senior year. Stopped hanging out, and eventually stopped messaging. I saw on his socials that he was with a different girl every month at college. My mother had been devastated, and I... well, I didn't think much about it.

"I couldn't let the night pass me by without coming to tell you how magnificent you looked today," he said, and I rolled my eyes at him even though I glowed under the praise. I was a whore for positive affirmation.

Mental note; talk to Dr. Handa about that.

"Thank you, Ajay. You don't look too bad yourself."

"Bought a suit just for this." He tugged on the cuffs of his sleeves; the fabric was rich and expensive, but he had wanted me to notice that.

"I'll bet you did." I smiled up at him, and we lapsed into silence as the bartender slid me my drink. I sipped on the bitter liquid.

"I hope you don't mind me asking, Mais, but what the hell are you doing?"

My heart was in my throat at his question. Of course, The Order wouldn't want us to disclose our deal with anyone else. I had to play the part; there was no room for the truth.

"How do you mean?"

"I mean, you're marrying some vampire, right out of high school? I always thought you were smarter than that."

He was staring at me, but I was not looking back. I was too afraid some shame would show across my features. Of course, that's what people would think. That we were stupid, but it made it easier to sell the *young and in love* thing.

"Crispin isn't just some vampire, Ajay." I hoped some of the acidity from my drink worked its way into my tone.

"Oh yes, the long lost bastard prince." His words dripped sarcasm.

"Is that what they're calling him?" I chuckled, wondering if Crispin would love that or hate it.

"I've never even heard of this guy, and suddenly you're married?" He tried again, his voice becoming darker and more accusatory by the second.

"I wasn't aware you needed informing." My eyes flicked to his finally, the irritation sparking in my chest, giving me the courage.

"I'm just worried about you, Maisie." He set his hand on my shoulder and turned me to face him. "Can he even take care of you?"

I knew the insinuation of the question. After five years, Crispin and I would never have to worry about anything for the rest of our lives. But rich hunter families were often very cliche and judgmental of people who seemed like a lower class to them. Trust fund baby, Ajay Harrison, was no exception.

"Are you ready for our dance, Princess?" Crispin's mocking voice came from behind me, and Ajay and I both turned to see him saunter over. Perhaps the words would have sounded endearing to anyone else; only I knew the truth.

He was dashing, I would give him that. His normally tousled blond hair was still messy but in a debonair 'I just filmed an action scene' way. His suit was exceptional, and I had tried not to let my eyes linger on him for more than seconds at a time.

"Of course." I smiled, setting my drink down at the bar.

"Pleasure to meet you, man." Crispin extended his hand, and Ajay reached to shake it. He was about the same height as Ajay, but for some reason, his presence seemed more looming.

"Crispin, this is Ajay, a friend." I introduced, gesturing between them.

"More than a friend at one time," Ajay added unnecessarily. I shot him a look and then noticed their hands were still joined in a never-ending shake.

"Ah, an old flame of my dearest Maisie's; she is quite the catch. Unsurprising that she would leave a few broken hearts behind her."

"Be a gentleman and give us a few more minutes, would you? I haven't seen her in a long while and want to finish my conversation with her." Ajay's tone was forceful, and my eyes went a little wider as I witnessed this archaic exchange.

They were having a pissing match in a ballroom.

"Sorry Ajay ole' pal, no can do." Crispin finally pulled his hand back as he stepped to me and wrapped his arm around my waist. "First off, I don't like your vibes. Secondly, if my new mother-in-law knows that I delayed a wedding coordinated event for even a second, she'll castrate me, and I have a honeymoon to enjoy, ya know? So if you want someone to talk to, go get your own wife."

He turned us both, dragging me toward the dance floor. I pursed my lips together, deciding I would save my biting words for when fewer people could hear them.

Three

Crispin

She was pissed. I could see it in how she looked at me through knitted brows.

"Are you serious?" she finally asked as "Too Marvelous For Words" by Ella Fitzgerald started playing. It was the song that her mother had picked as *'our song.'*

"You're not seriously mad about *one-hundred-dollar-hair-cut*-bro, are you?" I asked as I started the dance that we had practiced one thousand times, almost unaware of the rest of the wedding guests.

What the hell could she be so mad about anyway? Unless she still liked that asshole, who had put her in an awkward position by insinuating there used to be something between them. Maybe there still was, and that's why she was angry.

"Are you like in love with him or something?" I kept my voice flat, ignoring the blossom of jealousy in me. I buried it deep down so that even I didn't know where it went.

She stepped on my foot, hard, and I grunted in pain. *Question answered, I guess.*

"Might I remind you that we are supposed to not only be married but appear in love? Meanwhile, you are picking a fight with Ajay. Can you focus on what we are supposed to be doing?" She hissed at me through gritted teeth.

"From an outside point of view," I pulled her in close, and she rested her head on my chest. "Me fighting with your ex might indicate that I was in love with you, but if you want the wedding suite yourselves later, just let me know. Put a sock on the door to tell me if he's..."

She smashed down on my foot again.

"Would you stop that? These shoes are brand new."

I spun her out to the count in my head, and when she came back, she elbowed me in the ribs. For a tiny human, she had a lot of force behind her assaults. I tried to focus on the dull ache of the blow instead of how her dress dipped low in the back.

"Just do what you're supposed to, Crispin. I don't need you putting your nose in my business. You keep your end of the deal, and I'll keep mine."

"For someone so worried about appearances, you could try a little harder to appear infatuated. Elbowing your one true love hardly seems like the best acting." I spun her again and pulled her back to face me. She attempted to step on my foot again, but I stepped back to miss it. It messed up my count, and we had to reorient ourselves as both of us tripped a little.

"Maybe if you were more palatable."

"So you're in love with a fancy suit guy? Where'd you meet?" If she was going to be an ass, then so could I. There was no point in stopping this train now. I could only ride it to the end of the line and see how far I could push her.

It fed something in me to see the rage in her eyes, to get to witness, little Miss Perfect, lose her cool. I liked to watch the edge of her calm mask chip apart before she had time to fix it. I wanted to destroy the facade until I discovered what was underneath, and I wondered if anyone knew she held the anger that I had seen in our frequent spats and disagreements.

"Come on, Mais. You can tell me. Did he give you the best money can buy? A cashmere blanket in the back of his Range Rover?"

She stopped dancing, and though we were very near the end of the song, we weren't done. Her jaw was clenched, her hands balled into fists at her side, and I saw my words break the mask a bit. I glanced around at people staring at us, some of their brows furrowing a bit in question. We were the only ones on the floor, so her stopping to glare at me was very noticeable. I closed the distance between us and put my hand on her chin to tip it up.

Her eyes held a warning, but I ignored it and crushed my mouth to hers.

Cheers and hollers went up around us as people clapped. Maisie opened her mouth, and I opened my eyes in surprise, not realizing I had closed them in the first place. Her eyes were also closed, but just as I thought to pull her closer, I felt her bite down on my lip, and not in a hot way. I pulled back and stared as she smiled out at the crowd, covering her mouth as if slightly embarrassed. She turned and gave me the same smile that I may have confused for lovesick if she hadn't almost broken the skin of my lip. She turned back to me and placed a chaste kiss on my cheek.

"Fuck you. Crispin."

She turned and walked away with her fake face fully painted back on.

I danced with my mom and aunts and even Jaggar's girlfriend, Fern. She had copper hair that turned bleach blond and was tipped in black. It reminded me of fox coloring, and as we danced, she smiled, flashing her fangs freely, which jarred me a bit. I chalked it up to her being drunk and returned her to her table as quickly as possible.

I sat in a chair, sipping on someone's leftover champagne, watching Maisie talk to my cousin. She had ignored me the best she could, barely looking at me during the speeches. Darcy's speech had choked me up a little, and he had full-blown tears. From the corner of my vision, I'd seen Maisie wipe her eyes when Trudy got up and spoke as the maid of honor.

"You shouldn't kiss people who don't want to be kissed." A voice came to me, and I turned as Briar, my brother's human girlfriend, sat down. "You're lucky Maisie didn't punch you in the face."

Briar was slightly more observant than the average person, and she would also know the deal between Maisie, me, The Order, and the Guild because Darcy was the only one I had told.

"Hello, Briar," I said, draining the champagne flute. "You want to talk about kissing people without permission?"

This jab was a callback to the first time she had kissed Darcy during our senior year. At the time, they were fake dating, and Briar had kissed him unexpectedly to make her tool of an ex jealous. Her ex, Morgan, who happened to be Maisie's cousin. Darcy hadn't fed in a while at the time, and I had watched in horror as he almost ripped her to shreds as his vampire came out in the hall of our school.

"Touché." She crossed her arms in the chair, following my gaze to Maisie.

"I went to the pharmacy last week to pick up some prescription stuff."

"Good for you?" I tried to make my tone as irritated as possible because I thought it was better than having a sappy conversation with my brother's bitchy other half.

"I didn't have to pay a dime. The pharmacist couldn't tell me why I suddenly didn't have a copay for anything. Should have been five or six hundred dollars."

"Does this story get more interesting?" I felt her gaze on me as I said the words, so I turned to look at her. Her eyes were narrowed in suspicion.

"You wouldn't know anything about that, would you, asshat?"

"I can't say I keep up with your medical journey, Grey." I turned back to stare at my wife.

I heard Briar's chair scrape back, and I smiled in victory. That was before I felt the soft press of her mouth to my cheek. I turned suddenly, my hand coming up to my face. She was flushed as I had ever seen her, rolling her eyes at me. My face also got warm as she opened her mouth, clearly struggling with the words.

"Listen, I know we have this asshole thing going, and that's fine with me, but thanks for... you know... whatever."

"Did you just say something about kissing people without asking?" I said, but I gave her a half-smile.

"I don't envy Maisie marrying the lesser of the Booker Brothers." She scowled at me and then returned a ghost of a smile.

Without meaning to, she spoke the truth. She was right about me being the lesser brother.

I watched as she walked to Darcy, who was waiting for her. He and I made eye contact, and he nodded to me, holding up a hand in a wave goodbye. In that gesture were a bunch of other things that can be spoken between siblings without words.

I nodded back and watched as they walked out of the ballroom together, Darcy's arm wrapped around her shoulders.

Four

Maisie

Crispin took showers that were wholly too long. I worried the entire hotel would run out of hot water. I'd peeked into the crack of the open bathroom door and saw him in the half-fogged mirror. He was just standing there looking absolutely miserable, staring into the void of his future as the water cascaded over his shoulders. I avoided looking any lower than his chest as I stepped back a bit, feeling like I was invading his privacy. That had been my intention, but seeing him look so...dejected had made me self-conscious about what I was doing.

"I also would like to take a shower. I'm all airplane gross," I shouted into the bathroom and walked away; a minute later, the water turned off.

The day after our wedding, we had an awkward meeting with representatives from OOVA and The Guild. They had told us what they expected for our week and a half honeymoon. Our social media feeds were to be filled with romance and pictures of an in-love couple on the best trip of their lives. We had been chastised for the tension displayed on our wedding day. Apparently, others had seen the disdain we hadn't tried that hard to veil. It was followed by a threat that if we couldn't sell this, their end of the deal would be revoked.

We'd both agreed, and Crispin had mumbled an apology to them under his breath. We'd flown to Seattle first class, and a private car had driven us to our luxury hotel.

Our honeymoon suite was beautiful, and I would have admired it under any other circumstances. An opulent king-size bed with a white down duvet sat on one side of the room. A stretch of a hallway went into another living room of sorts with a small dining table and some couches. The bathroom had a spa shower and a large copper clawfoot tub with an assortment of the hotel's product offerings next to it. There were three arrangements of flowers, a fresh fruit bowl, and the mini fridge was no doubt stocked with fancy snacks and drinks.

We had it to ourselves for a week and a half, compliments of The Guild. They'd also booked us for a couples massage the following day. I couldn't decide if it was a *fuck you* or a kind gesture.

Crispin came out with a white bath sheet wrapped around his waist as he towel-dried his hair.

"All yours." He gestured to the open bathroom door.

I scooped up my pajamas and toiletries and went into the bathroom without a word. I shut the door all the way in case he got the urge to be nosy like I had.

I eyed the bathtub and the bottle of bubbles and oils. But baths were celebratory, and I felt like vomiting. I set my bag next to one of the double sinks that Crispin hadn't claimed. His things were all rolled and organized into a leather pouch with different pockets. I unrolled it and snooped some more, amazed at his organization.

A bottle of *Versace Eros* was tucked neatly into one of them, and I took it out to smell it. I hadn't realized that Crispin had a signature fragrance until that moment, but now I recognized it as the scent that lingered on him for the time we had been together. I tucked it back where it went as my fingers grazed all his other toiletries, stopping on two nail polishes. I took out the OPI bottle and read the name: *Kyoto Pearl* and a matching base coat. Also, a Crispin signature. His nails were always well-manicured and painted the same pearlescent white. I just now realized he hadn't worn it for the wedding.

Crispin was a fuck boy at first glance. Six foot something with blond hair that occasionally hung in his eyes. He worked out a lot, and with or without a shirt, wasn't horrible to look at. He wore diamond studs in his ears and a delicate gold chain at his throat that I never saw him without. Style-wise, he was relaxed but always put together, and now, staring at his meticulously packed toiletry bag, it all was adding up. He'd brought his own blow dryer, for goodness' sake. No wonder he always gave off 'barely tried glamor' man vibes.

I huffed a laugh, put his polish back, and walked to the shower to turn it on.

I silently apologized to Crispin for criticizing the length of his shower. The spa shower was like an experience I never wanted to leave. After washing the airplane off me, sudsing my hair, and shaving, I sat in the three streams of water for several minutes.

When I finally came out, dressed in my striped pink pajamas, I stopped dead, seeing Crispin lying in the bed, flicking through TV channels.

The part I was trying my damnedest to ignore was that he had a medical pack of blood in his hands. He'd stuck a straw into it and sipped on it like a juice box. My stomach rolled in rebellion. Of course Crispin drank blood—He would have to. But knowing something and seeing it with your own eyes was completely different. I found I was disgusted watching the deeply colored liquid move its way up the translucent straw.

"I ordered us chicken caesar salads and coffee for dinner. If you want something else, you can call room service. I got you an iced espresso with some honey and cream."

I still stared, or glared at him in the bed, talking around a straw full of blood. "What do you think you're doing?" I folded my arms across my chest.

"Waiting for food. The mini fridge is also stocked with blood, so I had some of that." He wasn't even looking at me, which only fueled my irritation.

"I mean, what are you doing lying in the bed?"

"I'm tired," was his reply, and I decided right there he was being dense on purpose. So I stood there and stared until he decided to acknowledge me.

His semi-wet hair was pushed back, and he was shirtless. I wondered if he was wearing clothes under the bed sheets, but refused to believe he would be naked. His mouth was quirked into a smile as if he knew I was growing increasingly upset. My suspicions were confirmed by the slight mischief in his blue eyes as he stared at the large TV mounted on the wall. He finally turned his head to look at me; eyebrows raised and an undeniable smile he was attempting to quell.

"You can't sleep in the bed." I tried again.

"Why not?"

I pursed my lips, wondering why he was now throwing a fit about this. He'd slept on the couch in the wedding suite the night of our wedding. And I'd been relieved it wasn't something we had to talk about.

"Because you slept on the couch last night and…."

"I'm not going to sleep on the couch for the next five years, Maisie." His face had lost its humor, and a hard edge lay there as if he were disappointed in my answer.

"You'll have your own bedroom in our house when we get home," I mumbled, less sure about myself now.

"And when we travel? Is it just the couch for me? No. I'm sleeping in this bed. It's as big as my room back home; we won't even be touching. You can sleep on the couch if you don't want to sleep here with me." He went back to flipping through channels as I made a growl of sorts in my throat to express my frustration.

It wasn't fair to expect him to sleep on couches while we were on our "show-off tour." I worried at my lip a bit, feeling the bloom of self-consciousness in my stomach, which was stupid. It was just Crispin and me here. I let out a long sigh and came around to the other side of the bed, where I had plugged my phone charger in.

"Not very gentlemanly," I complained as I stared at my screen and he grunted in response.

I held up my phone to take a high selfie of us both. Crispin didn't miss a beat as he turned and blew a kiss to the camera. I posted it on all my socials with the caption "landed and are enjoying the honeymoon" with a heart emoji. I tagged Crispin and changed my name to Maisie Booker-Pope on all my platforms.

Crispin and I had changed our statuses to married yesterday at the same time, and I scrolled through all the congratulations messages on both posts. Briar had posted laugh and dead face emojis on every single update we posted.

When I got back, I was going to strangle her.

A knock on the door down the hall, followed by an announcement that our food was just beyond had Crispin bounding out of bed. He was not naked, in fact, but wore gray sweatshorts that hung slightly below a band of boxer briefs. A woman wheeled a tray in with a large bowl of beautiful-looking salad and plates covered in silver domes. Crispin ran to a pair of discarded pants, making small talk with the young woman. She stared at the planes of his toned chest when she thought he wasn't looking, and I raised an eyebrow in her direction. She saw me, and her gaze dropped away from mine to the floor instantly.

Finally, he pulled out some cash to tip her and thanked her as she left.

I stood to get myself some food, but Crispin waved me away as he prepared both plates piled with fresh salad topped with grilled chicken. I watched him taste both coffees, which were in frosted glass cups with glass straws.

"I also got us a piece of a turtle chocolate layer cake to split," he said as I watched an infomercial about laundry hampers. "I thought it would make a great Instagram post." The last bit was said in a mock tone, and I wasn't sure if he was mocking me or The Guild and The Order.

He delivered a plate and a glass full of iced coffee to me and took one to his side. We silently ate our salads on the bed, watching a woman fold and unfold collapsing laundry hampers. Crispin took the credit card out that The Order had given us both and ordered one while we watched.

"What's our address?" he asked and I repeated the address back to him. "Thank you so much, Darling. Oh yes, we just got married. We are in our honeymoon suite watching your excellent TV spot," he said to the person over the phone as I rolled my eyes.

I took our plates to the cart and brought back the layer cake with two forks. I stretched out, setting it at the bottom of the bed as Crispin followed suit, putting his phone in front of us. We were so close, shoulder to shoulder, and he smelled good, like his damn cologne. I wish he smelled bad.

I was supposed to just sleep next to him with him smelling so good? Without a shirt? How the hell was this supposed to work?

However, the picture of him sipping blood like a juice pouch made me recoil from any of his appeal.

"How do you know what coffee I like to drink?" I asked to distract from our proximity before I would let him take a picture of us like this. Because then, every time I saw it, I would think of how good he smelled and just maybe how his mouth would taste after he drank blood.

"Maisie, I've hung out with you for like a year, dude. I know what coffee you drink." He rolled his eyes and jerked his chin toward the camera.

I picked up a fork and scooped up some of the decadent cake; reaching over, I placed it in his mouth as we both made a goofy face at the camera.

He posted it on Instagram, and the caption read:

Chocolate Cakes and Honeymoons 15/10

After cake photo ops and watching our fill of laundry hamper sales, we laid down awkwardly next to each other. At least, I hoped he felt at least a fraction of the tension I did as I looked at the ring that Crispin had put on my finger the day before.

The engagement ring he had given to me the day of graduation. He'd set it in my palm unceremoniously and told me I could wear it if I wanted to. I hadn't even put it on until the morning of the wedding. I'd kept it hidden away in my jewelry box, not wanting to look at it.

The Guild had provided me with the gold riveted band I had presented to him, so I stared closely at the one The Order had picked for me. The longer I stared at it, the more confused I became. The wedding band and the engagement ring were yellow gold. The band had obviously been crafted to match the intricate etching of the band of the ring, but the engagement band was scratched. I took it off and held it to the light. The deep red stone wasn't a ruby; the color was a bit flatter. Garnet, probably, and I saw the flash of an engraving on the inside as I pulled it closer to my face.

So Well As You

"What the hell does that mean?" I voiced aloud, the irritation building in my stomach that I had been gifted a ring that had belonged to someone else. Had it been bought at a pawnshop? I slid it back on my finger and sulked a bit.

"What the hell does what mean?" Crispin finally glanced over from whatever he was looking at on his phone.

"OOVA bought a secondhand ring with another person's damn inscription inside it, and the stone is a garnet, for heaven's sake. You'd think they could afford a new wedding ring with all the money they poured into the wedding. Who buys a gold and garnet wedding ring?" I held my hand up, staring as I rambled on. "Not that it matters, a stupid ring for a stupid marriage."

"Stupid ring for a stupid marriage," Crispin chuckled, and when I detected a roughness in his voice, I turned, but he was back to his phone screen, seemingly unbothered by my outburst.

So I turned off my bedside lamp and turned away from him, wishing he wasn't here so I could cry some more.

Five

Crispin

If I'd thought for a minute Maisie couldn't get any pinker, I was wrong. As she talked to the barista, I watched her from the comfortable leather chair inside the hipster coffee shop. A pink plaid skirt swirled around her ankles, and a pink button-up was tucked and tied up over it. Pink sparkling earrings and a couple of pink bangles on her wrist. Even the shoes she wore to walk around the city were fashionable pink Adidas.

Maisie was petite and short, probably not even five foot two inches. She had shoulder-length curly rich brown hair and bronzed olive skin that was just starting to lose its tan. Dark brown eyes the color of fresh black coffee and a beauty mark to the left of her nose and above the right side of her lip. Her perfectly straight white teeth were kept that way by a retainer she wore at night.

I had realized the retainer thing when her snoring had woken me up that morning. Then I realized we had drifted closer together than I imagined we would have, but I managed to get out of bed before she woke up and noticed. No reason to give her any points about my sleeping on the couch argument.

My phone buzzed in my pocket, and I took it out and opened a message from Darcy.

Darcy: *You both still alive?*

Crispin: *Who do you think would go down first in a fight?*

I chuckled as bubbles appeared and disappeared and then came back.

Darcy: *You would. She'd kick your ass for sure.*

Crispin: *I'm offended.*

Darcy: *Seriously though, you okay?*

I answered by sending him a picture of the coffee place, which was no answer at all, and I'm sure he would point it out. I didn't know the answer to the question, and I didn't lie to my brother if I could help it.

"Hey," a female voice said as I looked up from my phone to see a girl about my age across the small coffee table in front of me. She had a piercing in each eyebrow, and her hair was a bright magenta.

"Hello." I smiled at her as she looked me over.

"You're kinda in my seat." She gestured to the couch I was slumped into.

Her tone was flirtatious and I reveled in the thrill of it. There was little else I enjoyed as much as I enjoyed flirting without consequence.

"Must have missed the sign when I came in." I leaned forward, resting my forearms on my knees.

"That's okay, if you just move over a little, I don't mind sharing." She walked around the table with a cheeky grin on her cute face. She was bold; I liked that in a person.

"I might let you, though my wife will be back momentarily with my coffee." I surveyed her features as I said this. Her eyes darted to the ring on my left hand and then back to my face, her lips twisting in confusion.

"I'm sorry, I... you don't look old enough to be married," she stammered, stepping back.

"He isn't." Maisie's voice finally came, and I glanced to where she had walked up.

"Wife, meet the girl who owns this chair, cute girl who owns this chair, my wife." I introduced them, sitting back, and the girl said hello before awkwardly trying to dismiss herself.

"No, please, I wouldn't dream of separating you from your favorite seat," I said, standing up and shoving my phone in my pocket. "Thank you, Darling." I took a cup from Maisie, not caring if it was mine. I leaned in to kiss her cheek but stopped before my lips touched her skin.

Walking out, I gave the coffee shop girl a wink before pushing the doors open. Once outside, Maisie snatched the coffee out of my hand and all but shoved the other one back into my empty palms.

"That was kind of cruel," she grumbled as we began to wander aimlessly on the streets of downtown Seattle.

"What part of it was cruel?" I quirked an eyebrow at her, but she didn't answer me. We just kept walking, and I wasn't entirely sure if she was following me or if I was following her.

Eventually, she stopped on the rainy sidewalk and held out her coffee cup for me to hold. She pulled out a pack of cigarettes, Lucky Strikes, with a gold circle around the label. Her hands were shaking a bit as she fumbled to get one out. She then retrieved a pink and gold gradient lighter. She lit the end and took a deep draw off it like it was going to save her life.

"It is cruel to flirt and pretend to be interested in a girl."

"Who was pretending? She was cute. I was just flirting, Maisie; lighten up."

"I don't want you to fuck this up for me, Crispin, because you don't care. Because this is all like a joke or a game. I need this to work, I need people to believe us if that is what The Guild and The Order want."

"What did you ask for?" I asked as she turned away from me, the anxiety written plain across her face.

Maisie wasn't the only one who had been snooping around in the bathroom the day before. Only instead of what lotion she was using, I found a bottle of anxiety medication with her name on it. The Princess was always so composed and put together. She never had a hair out of place or a piece of lint on her clothing. She gave off a 'screw you' elegance that I had known had to be an act, but the woman before me now was kind of a mess just like the rest of us. It was comforting and unnerving at the same time.

"It's none of your business.""I feel like you are making it my business by demanding that I act how you want me to." The store of anger was an easy reach for me as I became irritated with her. "You've been kind of a drag the last few months, to be honest."

"Sorry my trying to act like an adult, and your childish ways of coping with things don't vibe." She drew in a mouthful of smoke with still trembling hands.

I could tell her I knew her secret, that she was hanging on by a thread. That she wasn't any better than the rest of us, than me. But it was an insult for a different time. I wanted to push her to rage, to fight me. I loved to fight with Maisie.

But I did not want to push her into a nervous breakdown.

"Well, I am going to find something to do to have fun; we can even take some romantic pictures for the cameras," I grumbled, pulling my phone out to look up what to do for fun in Seattle.

We ended up in Pike's Place Market. We got yet another cup of coffee when we got there, and a sandwich for an early lunch.

"Why don't you buy a new dress for dinner with the stuck-up vampires we have to go to?" I asked as we passed a retro clothing store.

We had two meet-and-greets with two vampire families during our *honeymoon*. The first was an affluent political family on Bainbridge Island, and another older family later in the week. Tonight, we were to go to David and Emily Steele's home. David Steele was at the forefront of Vampire Rights. He went to all governmental meetings. He was like one of the biggest Vampire politicians of my parent's age.

"What does a vampire politician actually do?" Maisie asked as we arrived at the famous bubblegum wall. I smirked a little at her general disgust of it, written on her face.

"What do you mean? They advocate for vampires." I shrugged.

"Advocate for what? I mean, what do you need advocating for?"

It wasn't a malicious question or even a surprising one. Hunters often knew nothing of the rights withheld from vampires for simply being born different.

"I guess that depends a lot on when you're talking about. Most recently, equal access to federally provided blood supplies, and the elimination of hunting non-threat vampires. But through the years, there have been other things. Vampires were classified as non-human, or once it was illegal for vampire couples to have children. At one time, Vampires were not allowed to vote on bills that affected them directly, or serve in certain 'high-risk jobs.' In the seventies, the United National Council upheld a law that vampire children couldn't go to school. It was quickly reversed, but children had to be homeschooled for two years, and each state had their own laws regarding college, so a lot of young adults were kicked out of programs, and when they went back, had to start all over again." I stopped myself before I rambled on.

Mandatory vaccinations and, at times, even clinical trials to cure Vampirism. Nothing had proven effective, obviously. There had even been times where medical care was only provided by certain doctors, and insurance would refuse to cover treatments for vampires. In the last four decades, we had come a long way. Vampires were treated like humans by most governments and could live practically everyday lives.

Darcy and I would sneak downstairs when we were little to listen to Mom and Dad talk about all of it when they thought we were asleep. Darcy had never let it weigh him down. He had always been better at it than I had.

"I feel really...ignorant for not knowing some of that." Maisie was looking at me when she spoke. My heart was in my throat at the sympathy in her eyes, like I was a gigantic jigsaw puzzle, and she had just started sorting the edge pieces.

"Yeah, well, I don't suppose they would teach it in, *how to be a hunter one-o-one.*" I turned away from the bubblegum wall, which I decided was terribly underwhelming.

Maisie followed me, and I walked back to the retro dress shop. I showed her to the door dramatically, as she walked in after me. I was glad we had stopped talking about things I cared about.

If I was going to survive as Maisie's doting husband who would divorce her without a thought in five years, I knew I didn't want her to look at me like she just had. Like she understood me. I'd fall in love with her that way. And love would definitely fuck everything up.

I did not want to fall in love with my wife.

Six

Maisie

I sat next to Crispin as two middle-aged vampires stared us down.

Emily and David Steele had a house like a museum, and that was saying something, given who I grew up around. David was an oily sort of man who might sell you a car for three times the price it was worth, or perhaps someone who sold dreams but had no intention of delivering the product. Emily, likewise, had sharp, severe eyes that seemed to see everything that transpired between Crispin and me. Though we were sitting close, and his fingers brushed mine affectionately every so often. His disdain at our act seemed to have disappeared, and now I was a bit freaked out by how easily he played the doting husband. There had been several times I went to look at him to find a syrupy, lovesick gaze on his face while he stared at me.

It made me want to punch him in the face, but I'd asked for this, so it wasn't really logical for me to feel that way. Perhaps it was that despite being on the mission of bringing vampires and hunters into a time of peace, I was still nervous around them.

I was surrounded, three to one, and I didn't even have a hunter blade.

Stop. I chastised myself. *This is exactly the kind of thinking that prevents peace. You're as bad as your uncle.*

My Uncle Fred and his oldest son had recently been incarcerated for crimes committed against a vampire family when they kidnapped Crispin's brother's girlfriend, Briar. They hadn't held my father's ideals of equality. In fact, if they could track down and kill every vampire that walked the earth, they would, threatening or not. I still remember the burning hatred in my uncle's eyes as I appeared at his trial and recounted the events that landed him and Adam in hunter prison. Luckily, his younger son, Morgan, was spared, but had a significant amount of probation and mandatory education to endure.

"So, Crispin." Emily's voice came across the table, breaking the awkward slice that weighed the room before.

"So, Emily," Crispin responded without missing a beat. He put a piece of chicken into his mouth, deliberately staring across the table.

"What color eyes would you say Maisie has?" The tone of the question was sweet and innocent, but I could hear the accusation that lay beyond it. Emily suspected that we were frauds and that this lovesick teenage act was all a front. If it made Crispin as defensive as it made me, he didn't show it.

"I would say they were brown. Or are you looking for something a bit more poetic?" He sat back in his seat and reached out to place his hand over mine. "The shell of a hazelnut, perhaps with lighter flecks scattered throughout? I could try to write a poem, but I'm afraid I was shit at it in high school, and I've not improved."

"What is she allergic to?"

It had turned into rapid-fire questions, and David smiled while he continued eating his food as if this were a normal occurrence.

"Penicillin." His reply came, and I tried to keep my tone neutral because that *was* true.

"What music does she like?"

"Most anything, not death metal or pop country."

My husband stared this woman dead in her eyes like she was not one of the more influential vampires in the world. I thanked my lucky stars; she wasn't asking me these questions because I realized I didn't really know the answers.

"Oh, such a romantic, Darling, the boy is absolutely smitten." She was mocking us again, and I felt my cheeks heat as I gripped my silverware tighter.

"So it seems," David said, taking a long draw from his wine glass.

"Surely such a romantic husband would have no trouble remembering the first time he laid eyes on his true love." She leaned in, folding her hands, and flashed pointed teeth in a predatory manner.

My breath had gone shallow as I stared at Crispin, my anxiety creeping up my throat, making it impossible for me to say anything.

"I'm not sure it was love at first sight for Mais, but it sure was for me."

Lies flowered so easily from his mouth it would be a wonder if I believed anything he tried to tell me from that moment on.

"Darcy and I were new to school, and we transferred part way through junior year, which was a nightmare." He waved his fork around as if this had all happened yesterday.

What a good damn liar.

"We fell in with the track and basketball guys right away. Erik, one of our good friends, was going steady with this girl, Trudy. Trudy's an absolute legend with a heart of gold. Anyway, she invited us one day to a soccer game after school. Not that she played, but she swore her best friend was incredible, so we went."

My anxiety took a back seat as I tried to determine if this was a real story or completely fabricated.

"Anyways, I couldn't take my eyes off Maisie the whole game. And I know what you're thinking, but it wasn't because the soccer uniform was irresistible. The unforms are incredibly unflattering, actually. However, Maisie played with so much passion I couldn't help but watch her."

"What position did she play?" Emily's question cut into the story, and I scowled at her.

"Oh, Mais always plays center forward. I think I've only seen her play goalie once, and that was a disaster."

I blinked away my surprise, trying not to let it overwhelm my face.

"Trudy introduced us after the game, but Maisie didn't look at me twice. I wouldn't be surprised if she doesn't even remember, but that was it for me. I've been chasing her around ever since."

"More like harassing me." My words came out, and Crispin let out a light laugh. Not a real laugh, which hurt my feelings a bit, but I didn't have time to dwell on the why.

I did remember the game. He was leaving out that he made a snide comment about those unflattering soccer jerseys, and I remember thinking it was such a shame he was an ass because he was so handsome.

"Well, what else are high school romances made of? It's positively perfect for a Netflix original." Emily cooed, finally letting it drop.

We finished dinner without any more berating. Emily and David bickered back and forth about the dates of an anniversary cruise. Crispin and I sat listening to them go at it, as you do when married people argue in their own homes.

"I like that dress," Crispin leaned in and whispered to me.

I looked down at the black velvet wiggle dress with lace edging on the V neckline. I didn't wear a lot of black, obviously. Even if I wasn't wearing pink, I was wearing other bright colors. The dress was a little...*vixen vampire,* and that's why I had picked it. The way Crispin's eyes had tracked over me when I stepped out of the bathroom was just a secret bonus.

"Tired of pink?"

"Would it matter if I was?" he asked, then scowled slightly at the couple across from us that was still in their back and forth.

"Nope."

"Good, that's what I like to hear." He sat back in his seat, withdrawing from our conversation. For a minute, it had felt a little like our old selves. Like the senior year before we had found out we were going to be married. Before this weirdness had settled over us. When we could bicker and banter and flirt because there was no way anything could come of it.

Because I was a hunter and he was a vampire, and I knew there were lines.

"What do you think about the progressive peace acts between The Guild and The Order, Maisie?" It was David who addressed me after a time of Crispin and I sitting in silence.

"How do you mean?" I asked, not wanting to seem as if the question completely dumbfounded me.

"Do you have any opposition to it?"

"I think you'll find my generation has much less objections. We were raised with less prejudice than even you were. It isn't a matter of whether vampires stop being hunted like animals and be allowed to live normal lives, but why they weren't at any point. Other than a few pockets of devout hunters who hold to the old ways, many younger hunters find it...sickening to think of killing peaceful vampires."

"But what is a peaceful vampire?" Emily interjected, and that wicked edge of trouble lingered in her face. "What if a teenage vampire kills someone on accident? What if a child vampire kills another on a playground? What if a man's wife dies, and in his grief, he goes to a vampire club and accidentally kills a feeder? Or what if vampires are loudly protesting the murder and devastation of our people? Are they not considered peaceful? What would be your definition?"

So there it was. A hunter surrounded by vampires and even Crispin stared at me, looking for my response. A response I didn't fully have time to craft.

"To the last part of your question, no. I do not believe vampires should be punished for protesting, and neither should someone be hunted for an accident. However, there are still consequences for accidental deaths, even when commited by a human."

"Ah, so vampires don't qualify as humans?"

That isn't what I meant, and she knows it.

Vampirism was a disease that changed a person's DNA. You could be born a vampire if you had vampire parents or you could be made into one by blood to blood exposure. Vampires were humans, there was no argument. They were just humans with a lifelong infection.

"Do humans killed on accident by vampires not count as victims?" I responded, my face heating.

"Let's bring out the lava cakes and not talk politics anymore. Emily, you can't expect these children to have the answers to life's big questions. These issues have plagued the world for centuries. Let them play their role."

The condescension in his voice slapped me across the face, shockingly blatant. It hit its mark, and I felt the wave of shame he had wanted me to feel. Perhaps Crispin had been right earlier, and I was privileged never to have had to think of these things before.

After a very tense dessert, we said our goodbyes and walked to the car waiting for us outside the large home. The night was colder, and I rubbed my hands over my exposed arms.

"I don't see how that could have gone worse," I said, stopping outside the dark sedan with tinted windows.

Crispin glanced at the front door cautiously. "It could have definitely gone worse. The wife was looking at you like she wanted to make you her dessert. I bet she's a vampire clubgoer. Especially because she mentioned it."

"What is a vampire club?"

"Like feeding clubs. Humans volunteer to be like live feeding bags. Normally, lots of drugs are taken by humans and then they're drunk by vampires."

"Why the hell would a human volunteer for that sort of thing?" I felt sick to my stomach at the idea of humans being drunk, open and freely, as loud music played. It was a grotesque image.

"Well," Crispin shrugged his sports coat off and draped it around me, talking as he adjusted it. "As you probably have heard, it feels good to be bitten. Like drugs with no health risks, really."

"Other than a vampire might accidentally kill you." I glared at him.

"Well, yeah, other than that."

"Other than death, there isn't really a downside then." I was nearly yelling as he held the lapels of his coat. His eyes shifted to the door once more before he suddenly pulled me in and pressed his mouth to the hollow of my throat.

I gasped, feeling the softness of his lips against my skin. I felt drunk on anger, confusion, and something more pleasant, but I soon realized what he was doing as I heard the door open. So I let my hand come up to where he had trapped me with his coat and rested my hand on his cheek. I focused on how mad and ashamed I was from dinner instead of how warm I was now.

Emily cleared her throat, and Crispin pulled away with a goofy grin plastered on his face.

Bastard vampire prince, my ass, the bastard prince of lies, was more like it.

“You forgot your to-go bag. I would be absolutely devastated to have to eat another cake tomorrow.” She held out a to-go box with her last name stenciled in gold on the side. My parents were well off, but we didn’t have doggy bags with our family name on them.

Crispin stepped forward to accept the bag, and we said one more goodbye to the woman I hoped never to see again. A heavy strangeness settled over Crispin and me as we climbed into the car and told the driver to take us to the ferry. I pulled Crispin’s jacket around me tighter, realizing it smelled like his cologne, and it was somewhat comforting against the cold and awkward silence that sat between us. It smelled warm, like cedar and vanilla, and something a little sharper...maybe green apple?

“I’m sorry I grabbed you, and....” He waved his hands around to signify something else.

"It's fine." I kept coolness out of my tone. "I'm sorry I was getting upset with you. I wasn't expecting to be surprised with all those questions. It's not your fault things are the way they are or that I don't know much about it."

"I don't know much about hunters either, to be fair." He sounded tired, and I watched him slump into the car's dark leather interior.

"Maybe we should like... talk about it?" I offered. "Then we won't be so blindsided next time. And I can memorize that *us meeting* cute story you made up."

His eyes shifted to me. I knew he hadn't made it up, but admitting that seemed intimate. Crispin only nodded, and we didn't speak for the rest of the car ride.

Seven

Crispin

"Yikes," Darcy's voice came over the phone. I was sitting in the bathroom on the ground, leaning back against the wall.

"Yikes– doesn't even cover it, Man. It was an absolute shit show."

"At least...." I heard my brother searching for silver-lining words. Darcy was the silver lining guy. I waited, hoping he could see something redeemable about this. "At least you remembered when you guys first met."

"And she was like a deer in the damn headlights, dude. She didn't remember at all."

"Did you want her to remember?"

I heard Briar's voice cackling in the background and then a string of words I knew would probably irritate me. Darcy chuckled and shushed her.

"Because why would it matter if she remembered or not?" he continued.

I half growled low in my throat. "Don't do the Doctor Phil shit, Darcy, please."

"Sorry, sorry. Anyway, I think talking about stuff is probably a good place to start. It's not like we were super educated on hunter culture, either. If you guys are supposed to be in love or whatever, you should probably have a crash course."

"Yeah." I was dramatically smacking my head into the wall behind me.

"I gotta go, but I miss you already." His voice was distant, but I'd kept him on the phone for twenty minutes to explain the entire night.

"You miss me? Gross." I stood up, reaching over to start the shower.

"Asshole."

"Bye."

"Bye."

I threw my phone into my towel on the counter and stripped down to get in the shower. I didn't take as long as I liked, but Darcy's suggestion to call my mom kept bothering me.

My mom had always felt like my real mom, even if we didn't look the same. I knew from the plethora of pictures around the house that I looked like my biological mother. With my blond hair, blue eyes and my dad's build, there was no faking that I wasn't the product of the Bookers.

When I was young, I used to take a picture of my mom and dad off the wall from the hallway outside my bedroom. I would sit in my bed with it and imagine what other ways I was like them. Mom and Dad always made a point of pointing things out. I smiled like my dad or got my wicked sarcasm from my mom. Was that true, or were they just trying to make sure I felt connected to people I didn't even remember?

The Bookers tried hard– harder than most adoptive parents. To make sure I had every opportunity to explore my lineage. Even if they disapproved, they let me reach out to my grandfather when I was twelve. He sent a response via his assistant in the form of an email, and the coldly typed words did not hide their meaning that he had no desire to be involved with me.

My mom blamed herself. I heard her talk to Dad late at night, sitting on the floor outside their door. She cried, wondering if they made the right choice by fighting for custody of me. She wondered if I would have been better off with my mom's parents. At twelve, it had cut me deeply; I'd taken it like she wasn't sure she wanted me. My parents loved me, but a constant guilt plagued my mom about what my life would have looked like being raised by rich assholes. Would I have had a better life?

I might have had more stuff, but based on what I witnessed of my extended biological family, including at the wedding, I would rather act like my parents than them-*entitled, insufferable assholes.*

I hit my mom's contact and dialed her number as I wrapped a towel around myself and brushed my teeth. She picked up before the end of the first ring.

"Crispin!" Her tone was happy and relieved, and I smiled against the warmth of it. I hadn't been gone long, but my mom was a worrier.

"Hey, Mom," I garbled around a toothbrush.

"Hey, Sweet, how are you? How is Maisie? How is the city? How was your dinner with that couple?"

"Geez, Mom." I spit toothpaste into the sink and wiped my mouth.

"Sorry, how are you?" She slowed her words, and I heard my dad laughing in the background.

"I'm good; the hotel is legit. The meeting with the vampires tonight was...well. I'd rather eat dinner with you guys any day of the week, but they sent us home with dessert," I rambled, leaning on the counter.

"How is the city? Are you having a good time together?" She volleyed another question at me before I had gotten done answering her previous.

"I guess we are having an okay time. It's not like... a vacation?"

"Dad wants to know if you bought Maisie flowers," she said, and I heard my father say something else that she chose not to relay.

"Bought her flowers?"

"Yes, when we were young, your dad and I visited the public market there, and there was a beautiful selection of flowers. He wants to know if you bought Maisie some."

"Tell Dad I'm not trying to romance her."

"He says he's not trying to romance her, Nolan." Then, after a brief pause, "I don't think he believes you for some reason."

My parents shared a laugh, the laughter of people in on a joke you weren't a part of—the laugh of best friends–of soulmates.

"Okay, well, it's been good chatting with you, Mom." I set the phone on the counter and put it on speaker as I pulled on clean clothes.

"Oh, we are just teasing, Honey," she said after their giggling had subsided.

"Love you guys." I opened the door to the bedroom.

"We love you too. Give our best to Maisie." Then a distant, "Love you, Son, remember the flowers." Came further away.

"Love you too. Talk to you soon," I said, hitting the end call button before locating where I had thrown my phone charger earlier.

"That's so cute that the bathroom is like your little family call center," Maisie said from where she was perched on the edge of the bed, channel surfing. There was more than a bit of meanness to her voice for reasons I was too tired even to try and decode.

"Yeah, well, at least I have a family that wants to talk to me."

It was the wrong thing to say. I knew that, but she had a way of jumping on my last nerve even when I was in a good mood. However, it shut her up, and I located my phone charger in peace.

Maybe Maisie's parents had texted her, but they had barely spoken to her at the wedding, and the only phone call she had taken was from Trudy checking in after we landed. I didn't know much about the Popes, but they didn't seem close or affectionate.

Once I plugged my phone in, I finally turned and really looked at Maisie. Her mouth was pursed into a tight line as the dim light illuminated her face with its changing tones. She was wearing velvet pajamas that looked like they cost more than my truck. The deep magenta color made the flush on her cheeks more prominent. I remembered my brother's words and took a deep breath to channel a little bit of Darcy.

"Sorry. That wasn't nice."

"No, but it was true," she bit out.

"Well, not all true things need to be said. I'm still working on that, but Darcy says it to me enough that I know I have a problem with it." I sat next to her and looked up at what she stopped on.

It was a Gilmore Girls rerun–the third and best season, in my humble opinion. She tossed the remote into my lap and sighed, crawling back on the bed to her side and settling in.

"You can change it."

"We can watch this," I said, scooting back as well and leaning against the headboard.

"You like Gilmore Girls?"

"Yeah, my mom watches it."

Lie. Darcy and I rewatch all seven seasons every year, starting in October.

"You're a Logan girl, aren't you?" She smiled at me, and that was all it took for my irritation with her to melt away. *Damn it all.*

"So that is what you think of me?" I mock scowled, reaching my hands up and resting my interlaced fingers behind my head. "I'm a Jess girly till the day I die, Princess. Was he a little toxic? Sure, but he loved Rory the most."

"Debatable." She smiled, her real smile, and it did more than just thaw me. My insides felt like they were emitting warmth.

"Don't start something you can't finish. I'll call my brother up right now, and we can get into this philosophical conversation if you want."

She laughed before settling back, and I couldn't help the feeling that I wanted to buy her some damn flowers.

She fell asleep while the TV was on. I watched her melt like ice cream, slowly sinking lower and lower into the bed until she was curled up and away from me lightly snoring. Which I was so glad to hear and use as ammunition tomorrow. Though to be honest, it wasn't a bothersome sound: just a reminder that she was there.

I turned the TV off so the noise wouldn't wake her and turned her light off on her side of the bed. I read a few news websites and a bit of the book we were reading in the family book club. It was some historical romance book my mother had recommended, and I sent a salty message about the count of the estate not having the balls to ask the woman to marry him. Then making a chess move in my mobile game with Erik, I flipped my phone over and turned my own light off.

Tomorrow I could be better. I would try harder to...not be myself. Even if Maisie drove me absolutely nuts, I didn't want this trip to be bad for her. She didn't deserve that, and I know I didn't need to be such a jerk.

Flowers and coffee it was, with absolutely no outside flirting.

Eight

Maisie

"Are you alright?" I asked Crispin as he pulled a card from his wallet that was definitely not the card The Order had given us. Was it his personal card? Why was he paying for the flowers with his own money?

"Why do you ask?" He scanned the rows of fresh bouquets of flowers.

This morning I had run into him at the gym in the hotel just as he was getting done and I was just starting. He had asked if I wanted to order some room service or if I wanted to go get some breakfast. Then after I worked out and showered he told me I looked nice. Then as we had coffee and bagels, he asked what I wanted to see in the city before we had to leave. He was being downright pleasant, and I was getting weirded out.

Even now in his tapered and cuffed khaki pants, with his knit cable sweater, waving his fingers over the flowers as if looking for just the right ones. He stopped at a pink bouquet and the man handed him a receipt with his card.

"Here you go." Crispin gave me the bouquet, and I held them to my face to smell.

"What's going on?" I asked again, though nearly distracted by the pink blooms.

He sighed and ran a hand through his ear length hair, pushing it back from his face. He flashed me a blue-eyed stare complete with a crooked grin and one eyebrow raised that would make weaker women swoon.

"What?" I asked.

"Walk with me," he said in some corny TV voice. We began to walk, and his mock confidence began to wane as he rubbed the back of his neck. "Listen Maisie, the thing is, whatever this is that we do." He pointed between us.

"What thing?" I was holding the flowers to my chest as if they might protect me from this conversation.

"Let's not do that; let's just be honest here for a second. The irritated argument thing we do, okay, it worked when we were friends, but it's not working out since...."

"Since we got married."

"Exactly." He sighed, thankful he hadn't had to say it. "Before, it was fun and flirty, but now it feels real. I don't mind arguing with you, but it feels like we've actually been at each other's throats for months. I didn't put you in this position, and you didn't put me here either. We both chose this for whatever reason." He stopped walking in the middle of the market, and his speech was now more hand gestures than words as he shook them in front of himself.

"What are you saying? That you want to...." I left the ending open.

"I'm saying that five years is a long time to be pissed at each other. At least if we are friends, the 'in love' part should be easier to fake."

"Aren't we friends?" I asked as something began to ache in my chest. Maybe it was the realization that I had been kind of awful to him for the past several months.

"We used to be, I think." He shrugged, and the emotion in me deepened. "I don't think this is all on you, Mais. I know that I've been an absolute ass. Not just in my regular way, either. I've been extra difficult, my frustration with this political bullshit has come out, and you've had to deal with it."

Damn the Booker brothers and their willingness to apologize.

My anger with him melted away, any remnant sloughing off like a winter coat when the sun came out. No matter my struggle to hang onto it, looking at him slightly unsure of himself with an awkward and heavy apology between us, I could not be upset—And I did try.

"Alright, " I agreed after my silence started to make him visibly uncomfortable. "We can do friends."

"Good." He looked relieved that I hadn't fought him on it. Part of me wanted to, out of self-defense. What if I trusted him or got close, and he hurt me? Or worse, what if after five years of being live-in best friends, he left me? And isn't that what I wanted?

We spent the rest of the afternoon going over hunter and vampire information. Crispin knew as much about Hunter life as I did about Vampire life– close to nothing. When I was younger, even though my dad was a vampire sympathizer, vampires had been portrayed as unfortunate side effects of nature. Like unstable bombs that needed to be delicately handled. Likewise, Crispin had a distaste for hunters; they were the natural opponents. I supposed he harbored some bad feelings from the end of senior year, when Darcy's girlfriend had been kidnapped by my uncle.

"Most hunters aren't like Fred and Adam."

"And Morgan," he reminded me, sticking his frozen yogurt spoon in my face as if to remind me of my other cousin.

"Take it easy on Morgan. He isn't so bad," I said, swirling my chocolate fudge on top of my coconut yogurt.

"He helped kidnap Briar." He frowned.

"Well, has he made all the right choices? No."

"He let his friends tag her locker like every day for months," he said, and I cringed, remembering the crude messages that had been painted.

"Okay, okay, so he's not going to win any humanitarian awards, Crispin. He's just... he's not like the rest of them. Sometimes you just do what your family does because that's all you know."

When we were kids Morgan had been a sweet boy, we had always played together. It wasn't until high school that he had turned into a jerk who parroted what my uncle Fred and cousin Adam said.

"I still don't like him."

"You don't have to." I rolled my eyes and tried to change the subject for a moment. "Who eats tart, unsweetened yogurt?"

"You're asking me that staring directly into my bowl, so the obvious answer is me."

"Seems like a red flag."

"Gummy worms and hot fudge are way more of a red flag, Darling. My tart yogurt with strawberries and Captain Crunch suggests a refined palette. Yours looks like a five-year-old slapped some stuff in there."

"Yours is like an old woman who is watching her figure."

"I am watching my figure. You think I look like this by accident?" He mocked himself, gesturing to his torso. Though there was nothing to mock. Crispin was handsome, confirmed by all the young women that oogled him wherever we went. He looked like he would be in an early 2000s young adult drama. He was all sweaters and sparkling eyes and good-smelling cologne and iridescent pearl nail polish.

"Where to next, Princess?" he asked, snapping my thoughts away from when he'd pressed his mouth to my throat in the driveway of those rich vampire's house. I cleared my throat and pretended to look into my yogurt to contemplate.

"I promised Trudy that we would get one of those strip photobooth photos before we left. She's doing some sort of scrapbook for me."

"I wouldn't deny Trudy anything." Crispin got up and threw his empty cup into the trash. He held his hand out for me to take. "Let's go find a damn photo booth."

The rest of the honeymoon went a lot smoother. Our handler from The Order, Jessica, called us the night before we were supposed to head to the airport.

"Your social media presence is acceptable but it could always be better," she mused, looking at something off-screen that neither I nor Crispin could see.

Jessica was a forgettable sort of woman. With mousy brown hair that she wore in a bun and a drab suit jacket that she repeatedly reused. I wondered if she had several of the same one or just put this one on every time she got on a computer meeting call. Her lips were thin and almost always pursed into an unpleasant frown.

"Do you want us to film a sex tape and upload it or what?" Crispin replied, and I snorted, grinning at him.

"Mr. Booker, I do not appreciate your attempt at humor. No, that will not be necessary. As long as you keep up the facade and put a touch more sincerity into it, I'm sure The Guild and OOVA will find it acceptable."

"Oh good," I said, and Jessica nodded, not noting the sarcastic tone.

"The next event you will be asked to attend is a prestigious Halloween party held by some of the influential Vampire Council members. It's a black tie costume party."

"What is a black tie costume party?" Crispin interrupted with his hand raised like we were in class.

Jessica sighed, exasperated. "I will send you the brief to your emails, but you will be required to go as a famous couple."

"I'll make sure the costumes are taken care of, Jessica. Don't worry," I assured, and she smiled at me. There was no doubt that she liked me better than Crispin. I don't think it was just because I was more compliant during these meetings. Like most hunters, she had a prejudice against him because of what he was.

"Thank you, Mrs. Pope."

"Pope-Booker," Crispin reminded her, and I swear I felt the heat of her irritation through the screen. I bit my tongue to keep from laughing again.

"Please reach out once you are home and settled so we can discuss your itinerary for after the party."

Once the call ended, Crispin snapped the laptop shut with an irritated growl in his throat. "I know we have to go along with all this, but I would also like to piss off both of these pretentious groups. They are essentially the same. The Order and The Guild–same bullshit old money politics wrapped in different paper."

"I know who we can go as." I smirked over at him.

"Go as?"

"To the Halloween party. I know the perfect famous couple."

Nine

Crispin

"Ready, Mais?" I called to the back room of the small condo that we were given as a 'home base' when we were in town.

It was very...white. The walls were white, the cabinets were white, the granite counters, the sheets on each of the beds, and the towels in the bathrooms. The pictures which, I was sure as I stared at them, were not white still held no trace of real art, and so they appeared white. It was all decorated in a modern style: vases with no flowers, bowls with nothing in them, and stacks of books that no one would read. It was like looking at one of the magazines my mother used to read while The Food Network was on for background noise.

The front door dumped into a hallway. To the left was the laundry room and bathroom; further down was the open kitchen, dining room, and living room. Beyond that was the hallway to the bedrooms where Maisie and I slept in separate rooms. At night, I dreamed about coloring with a black Sharpie on the walls.

It was sterile and not like a home at all. Though I supposed it wasn't.

Maisie came into view, and she was already fidgety. This wasn't a good sign, as her fidgeting almost always seemed to give way to insurmountable anxiety.

She wore a pink minidress with puff sleeves and pink high-top sneakers. She pulled at the gold necklace at her throat, which held a pendant of some saint. She wore it every day, though I knew she wasn't catholic.

"You okay?" I raised an eyebrow in question.

"Sure, fine." She nodded and looked for her handbag before finding it on the back of a white chair.

"You seem...." She glared at me, a warning in her eyes about my choice of words. "Fucked up." I chose to ignore her warning, and she frowned.

"It's just my parents' house. What is there to be worried about?"

So she was worried.

"I thought you were worried about going to my parents' house. Briar is going to be there after all." I watched her shoulders sag in relief a bit. Briar was a pain in the ass, but she was our friend, and I thought it might make Maisie more comfortable to know she would be present.

"I can handle Briar," she promised.

Lunch with the Popes and dinner with the Bookers before we were on a plane again in three days to go to the Halloween bash of the freaking century. We'd returned to town two weeks ago, but with all the meetings with Jessica and catching up with our families, I felt like we couldn't catch our breath. I wondered if this is how it would be for the next five years.

We backed my truck out of the spot as Maisie picked at the hem of her dress. The poof of the sleeve was a little comical in comparison to her stature. I turned on the next episode of a hunter podcast we had been listening to. We had each picked a podcast we enjoyed, Maisie on hunters and me on vampirism and we were taking turns listening. The unfortunate thing was that the episode I put on was about killing a vampire if the need arose. The man said it with an air of arrogance that caused anger to flicker within me.

Often, hunters spoke about vampires this way. Like they would live peaceably with us as long as we didn't get out of hand. Maisie reached forward and shut the radio off. Her breathing sounded slightly labored, and she stared intently out of the front window. I didn't know what to say, so I didn't say anything at all. I was too stupid to help but not stupid enough just to say whatever popped into my head.

However, I watched as her knee began to bounce up and down and she rubbed the gold pendant at her throat, and the closer we got to her parents' house the worse it became. Her knuckles gripped the fabric of the seat, white and rigid. Her normally flushed cheeks seemed pale.

The Pope's house was only about fifteen minutes away compared to my parents, who lived about forty minutes away now, in the same town where Maisie and I had gone to school. Apparently, they had paid money for their daughter to go to a school in a smaller town so she would have a better chance of being taken care of. Maisie had told me they wanted to send her to a private school, but she refused to go.

This had shocked me as Maisie was a chronic people pleaser, and her parents seemed to be at the top of her *must please at all costs* list.

We pulled in, and she finally spoke in a sort of harsh whisper, "You can go in." Her eyes were closed as she leaned her head against the headrest, but her fingers tapped an incessant rhythm on her knee. "You can tell them I'm on the phone or something."

Yeah, right, I'm going to go in and meet your parents who have you scared shitless all by myself. That is what I thought but did not voice.

Instead, I got out, walked around to her side of the car, and opened her door. She didn't move or look at me until I reached out and put my hand just above her knee. She jerked a little bit, and I pulled my hand away, lowering it to my side with a shuffle and a slight heat in my cheeks. I wished I could have not felt so self-conscious about my actions at that moment.

She stared at where my hand had been, and I cursed silently, seeing the tears that had formed in her eyes. I was terrible at this.

"What can I do?" I shrugged, sticking my hands in the pockets of my slacks.

"I don't know," voice hollow and nearly angry. "Just leave me alone." Her fingers tapped away, never stopping.

"Well, I can't do that."

Her eyes finally lifted to meet mine, and I saw the shame in them. I recognized the feeling of being trapped and not wanting someone else to see you that way. I'd felt it too many times when I experienced the thirst that lurked inside me, when I tested the limits of my tolerance, either on purpose or simple neglect. I wondered if this thing– this anxiety– clawed at her the way my cravings clawed at me in those moments. The shame of it potentially becoming someone else's problem.

"I don't know exactly what you have goin', Maisie, but I know it's hard on you. So if you want me to tell you I've got your back, that nobody is going to fuck with you while I'm around, or that we can leave the minute you want to. I can tell you all those things and mean them. I can also shut the hell up if you just need me to sit here, but I will not leave you alone right now. Maybe that's not what you need, hell if I know, but it's what I've decided."

She smiled a bit, and I nearly sighed with relief. She was still worrying at her lip, and I wondered if it might split open if she continued like that. An image of my tongue against her mouth to devour the evidence of her worry sent a shiver through me as I cast the idea away, disgusted that I had just offered to help her, and now I was thinking of how her blood might taste. Or was it her mouth? It was best not to think of either.

"Well, nobody will mess with you except me, and probably Briar, but she fucks with everyone." I reached out again and gently put my hand where it had been before, firmly enough that she would feel the sincerity. She didn't pull away, but she didn't look very comfortable either, so I didn't let it linger there long. I patted her good-naturedly— feeling like my dad after I'd just lost a big game. I stood patiently in the truck's doorway until she moved to get out what seemed like ten minutes later.

"Hey, Crispin," she said as I offered my hand to help her out.

"Yep?"

"You need to let my parents fuck with me. I don't think you're going to like it, but I need you to just...not say anything."

"I already don't like that."

"I know how you are. I don't need you to defend me."

"If that's what you want. I can behave." We walked up a long cobblestone pathway to the door.

"I'll believe that when I see it," she said as we stood before a set of massive gray double doors,

and she reached out to push the doorbell.

The food was like some fine dining experience, and the house was like a museum. Not a thing was out of place. Much like our condo, some decorations looked staged. Even the couches appeared as if they shouldn't be sat on. No sign of people living in the Pope's house. It was also enormous, which I remember Briar mentioning with distaste once or twice. The long tour that Maisie's mom, Helena, had taken me on was daunting. I felt like if I wandered away from her, I would be lost.

I stared at the meal before me, which was served to us by a woman named Mariel. She was introduced as their private chef and then promptly disappeared back into the kitchen. It did not escape my notice that Maisie called her by her name, and the two seemed to share some sort of closeness. Maisie relaxed a bit when the woman came out, and their short exchange seemed genuinely tender.

On my plate was a pear and cheese quiche. The cheese had been named in the description but I could no longer remember it. On the side was a cucumber shaving and some grapefruit and a single stalk of asparagus with dressing drizzled over the top. Mariel had explained it was a salad. I stabbed the cucumber curl with my fork and tried to get it into my mouth without drawing too much attention to myself.

"So, Jessica has been keeping us updated with your progress," Maisie's father, William, said.

"Oh?" Maisie asked, slicing the quiche delicately and taking the tiniest bite off her fork.

She had transformed as soon as we had come through the door. She was stiffer and more formal. Over the past couple weeks, she had relaxed a little in my presence. Even at school, she hadn't been this uptight, but I saw her now straining to be everything they wanted her to be, and it irritated me.

"What has she shared with you?" I asked, spearing a section of grapefruit. Maisie sat next to me at the table, and her hand, which was in her lap, moved over and gently smacked my knee.

"Oh, nothing to worry yourself too much about, son."

Nope, I didn't like him calling me that at all.

"Well, if I shouldn't worry about it, it shouldn't be a problem for you to tell us, William." I put the grapefruit in my mouth and earned another sturdier smack.

The man stared me down from across the table, and I stared back. My father taught me never to look away from someone who was trying to make me feel inferior, and I thought William Pope may have been doing just that.

Maisie's parents hadn't asked how she was. Hadn't asked how the trip went, if she had fun. Her mother had said hello, made a comment about Maisie's shoe choice, and then asked if I would like a tour of the house. When William had come into the dining room from his office, he had said hello to us both and sat down. Other than complimenting Mariel on the neatness of the plates, he hadn't said anything. Was this how Maisie grew up, or was the dynamic just off because I was there?

"Jessica has mentioned you are less willing to cooperate with reasonable requests than my daughter is," he said finally. "Though I'm sure we can all chalk that up to the nerves of your...arrangement."

I felt like I was in the damn twilight zone.

"You can chalk it up to whatever makes you most comfortable, sir." I smiled at him as he frowned. Maisie's hand was on my leg now, and she squeezed my knee. I looked over at her, trying not to show that I did feel a little guilty for failing so miserably at her instructions. I needed to be a better friend to her at this moment.

"This is probably one of the most interesting salads I've ever had, Mrs. Pope. Thank you for having us over for lunch." I tried for a tone of politeness that I wasn't feeling.

"My pleasure," Helena responded. "Oh Maisie, what will you and Crispin go to Dietrich's party as?" She changed the conversation like someone who was born to do it.

"We haven't decided yet. I've ordered a few options, we just need to narrow it down," Maisie said seamlessly, like it wasn't a blatant lie.

"Unfortunately, your father has an important meeting to attend, or we would fly out and go too. It's one of the most important parties of the year."

"You're going to the Bookers this afternoon?" William nearly interrupted his wife.

"Yes, for dinner." Maisie nodded.

"I enjoyed talking with your adopted father, Nolan, at the wedding." He pressed on, and instead of shooting him an irritated look, I cut into my quiche. "He seems like a down-to-earth sort of man."

What the fuck did that mean?

"He's a very good dad." I kept my voice as neutral as I could manage.

"I'm sure. He seems very capable despite the circumstances."

I saw Maisie stiffen in her chair as my anger flared. I choked it down for her sake, and I heard the click of my teeth grind together. "I couldn't have asked for a better one."

"I do hope you had time to visit the fitness room in the hotel you went to Maisie dear. I made sure there was one available to you. You wouldn't want all your training to go to waste," Helena said.

It was assault after assault while the two people seemed as if nothing was wrong. There was no warmth at the table. Despite it being set to perfection with some fancy-ass food–there was no love that I could feel. Instead, it was like they were going through a checklist of everything Maisie and I were supposed to be doing correctly.

"Maisie and I both got to use it," I chimed in, still pushing a polite demeanor. "I've seen Maisie play sports, but she works out like a mad woman. She could kick my ass, I'm pretty sure."

"That's what she was trained for. Just in case there was ever a need for it, of course, you understand," William said, and I looked at him, my mouth slightly open, unsure how someone could say so many wrong things.

"Maisie was always the best in her class," Helena said, and I did sense a bit of pride in her tone then, but only regarding Maisie's accomplishments.

I hadn't interacted with the Popes very much before we got married and then hardly at all at the wedding. I had clung to my parents and Darcy like a shield. I hadn't made it a priority, and now that I was here, I wasn't sure I ever would.

"Maisie tells me you both met in Florida?" I continued. I wished Darcy was there; he was so great at carrying on a casual conversation with people he didn't like.

As Helena recounted the events that led her and William to fall in love, I was grateful that the focus had been shifted away from us. Though every so often, I would catch William staring at me. He seemed as irritated with me as I was with him.

When we left and the Popes shut the door behind us, I let out a loud and mocking laugh as Maisie stared daggers at me. Not once had the conversation changed to be any less distant, accusatory, and bizarre.

"What the actual hell, Maisie?" I ran my hand through my hair as I walked ahead of her. "No wonder you are such a jerk sometimes."

"Hey!' she exclaimed in protest. "They were having an off day. I don't know what was going on with my dad."

"They always treat you like that?" I stopped and turned to gauge her face when she answered.

But she didn't respond, and she avoided my gaze, which was answer enough.

Ten

Maisie

My father did not like Crispin, and Crispin did not like my father.

JUST perfect.

We were only a month married, and already, my husband and the man who raised me hated each other's guts. The way my dad looked at Crispin when he called him *William* was almost comical now, but I thought his head might have exploded.

After my parents, we'd gone home and worked out in the small clubhouse gym, and then I had taken a shower and a forty-five-minute nap. Crispin hadn't pushed me for more answers about my parents— Only ran and trained with me and then left me alone.

The sound of the truck's electric window interrupted my remembrance of the most unfortunate lunch I had ever had.

"Just out of curiosity," Crispin asked from the driver's seat. "Exactly how many cigarettes will you need to smoke?"

I inhaled, but instead of drawing the smoke deep into my lungs, I blew it into the window of the truck and flipped him off. He rolled it up without another word.

Honestly, I dreaded the Booker house nearly as much as I dreaded going to my own. I don't know why I agreed to do both in a single day, but my social battery was already drained, and we still had more to do.

The Bookers were kind people, and that almost made it worse. Kind people had a way of wiggling things free that you had previously secured away, where they could no longer emotionally torment you. At least my parents were predictable. They were focused on my actions and my future. They wanted to make sure this marriage would look good on them so they could use it to further their standing with The Guild. They would leave me and my emotions alone as long as I behaved.

I walked to the front porch and opened an old espresso can, and dropped the butts of my smokes into it before walking back to the truck. Wordlessly, I pulled myself up inside and buckled up, punching the radio onto whatever station was first so Crispin didn't make some snide comment.

However, the bastard reached out and turned it down anyway.

"You good, Smokey?"

"Fine."

"You sure because I can call my parents and re-schedule."

"No." That wasn't fair. I'm sure they wanted to see him, and we would be gone again for another couple of weeks.

"I can just go," he questioned me, the car still in park. "You can go...take a bath or scream into the abyss? Maybe read one of those trashy cowboy romances you horde on your e-reader."

"You're such a damn snoop." I turned to look out the window, my cheeks reddening. I did have a cowboy addiction. I found one of said novels in my mom's donation box when I was seventeen, and since then, I had been addicted.

"Maybe you can give my mom some recommendations. Even better, maybe you can pick the next book for our family book club." His tone was teasing, and I tried to fight the small smile that bubbled to the surface.

He turned the music up and allowed me silence for the entire drive to his parents' house.

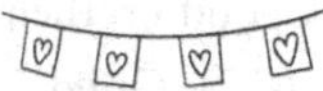

We walked to the door. Crispin looked at me as if I might lose it at any moment, but I didn't feel much anxiety, only dreadfully tired.

He had picked up a bouquet of white alstroemeria for his mom yesterday. When he went to pick one out for my mom, I told him she hated fresh flowers because of the mess. He'd scowled but put them back upon my insistence.

When we got to the door, I stopped so he could knock, but he did not. Instead, he opened the front door and helped himself inside. He set the flowers down on a side table and shed his thin windbreaker and shoes, tossing them haphazardly on the carpet. I looked after him, horrified.

"You don't have to take your shoes off," he offered, picking the flowers back up and motioning for me to follow him inside after I shut the door.

"Heyo, where's my welcome party?" he yelled into the house. Several seconds later, I heard heavy running footfall. Darcy appeared from around the corner.

Crispin had a split second to toss the flowers to me, which I barely caught as his brother tackled him to the ground, and they each began to try to pin the other to the carpet. I watched, unable to decide what to do with the flowers clutched against my chest as they rolled further into the living room, bumping couches and hurling nonsensical insults at each other.

"You'll get used to it." Briar's voice came from behind me, and I was slightly startled before relaxing.

"Do you?"

"No, actually you don't. The savagery of sibling love makes no sense to us, lonely only children." She smiled a bit, and something about her seemed softer than it had been a few months ago at the end of senior year. Her hair was green now and cut into a short bob, but her smile seemed less laced with venom.

"Savagery indeed." It was Mrs. Booker who spoke up, coming into the room. "Boys, you are going to break something, please."

"Hey, Mom!" Crispin said as Darcy let him out of a headlock. He stood up and walked to hug her.

"Hey, my boy." She squeezed him back tightly, and as she pulled back, I saw the glisten of tears in her eyes. "I missed you. I can't wait to hear about everything: the hotel, the food."

"Sleeping in the same bed as your centuries-old enemy," Briar added.

"Well, maybe we don't need details on that." Mrs. Booker laughed.

"Oh, I do," Briar pressed. I shot her a glare, and she grinned in victory.

"Easy." Darcy came and wrapped his arms around her and bent down to kiss her cheek. "I thought I told you to behave."

"Maisie, it's so lovely to see you, too!" Mrs. Booker interrupted, and as she came in for a hug, I held out the flowers in my hand. For some reason, I felt like if she hugged me, I would cry.

"These are for you, Mrs. Booker. They are not from me, from Crispin. He picked them out... I mean." I stumbled over the words, sounding as if this were the first social interaction in my life.

"Don't let anyone say you aren't articulate," Briar said, and Darcy's hand slid up to cover her mouth. I rolled my eyes as Darcy mumbled an apology on her behalf.

"Nice hair, Briar. Who are you supposed to be, the ghoul of diabetic's past?" Crispin cut in, but there was no malice behind it, and Briar smiled.

"Oh, those two will be at it all night if we let them, and please call me Kat." Mrs. Booker said, handing the flowers to Darcy. "Honey, take these and put them in a vase for me. I'm going to give Maisie a tour of the house."

She ushered me back to a staircase that led up to three rooms and a bathroom. First was Crispin's Room. She opened the door, and I smiled at the lack of privacy. Everything looked like I imagined it did when he left. A TV off to the side and a gaming monitor. A made bed and a desk with a computer. Posters of bands and an alarm clock on a nightstand.

"It's clean." I marveled, and Kat laughed. It made me smile because there was a gentleness to it.

"Yes, Crispin keeps himself very clean, but he's always been our messy one. Nolan always said it was because he was too creative to be tidy." She shut the door and moved around to Darcy's room, the bathroom, and the spare room. Her and Nolan's room was downstairs, and as we passed a hallway, she stopped in front of two pictures stacked on top of each other. One was of a couple holding a baby, and the other was of the same couple, just a little younger and on a beach.

"These are Crispin's parents," she explained. I focused on the pictures more, realizing Crispin looked a lot like his mom, but the smile on the man in the first one looked familiar to me, too.

"You guys were friends?"

"Liza and I were best friends." She nodded.

"I'm sorry you lost them." I didn't dare to look at her as I said it. Instead, I stared closer at the baby in the second picture.

"Thank you." She moved past the pictures as I followed.

She showed me the master bedroom and bathroom. Then we passed back by the living room and kitchen.

"The dining room is in there, but we ordered a bunch of pizza, so we won't eat there tonight. I thought less formal might be more comfortable. Do you like Monopoly?" She talked fast like Darcy sometimes did. They had too much to say but not enough time to say it.

"I haven't ever played, actually," I admitted.

"Oh, goodness," She put her hand on my shoulder, and I had to try not to shrug it off. "It's about to become a war zone."

The Booker's were a lively bunch. There wasn't a single moment of silence. They laughed as much as they talked, and when the pizza finally came, everyone crowded around the boxes and stacked pieces on flimsy paper plates before heading to the living room.

It was chaos.

"What kind of person hasn't played Monopoly?" Briar asked as she handed out our little game pieces. I was assigned a tennis shoe and turned it over in my palm to examine it.

"I didn't have siblings, and my parents didn't play board games much. I don't know?" I shrugged. "Are you very interested in the board game history of my life?"

"Not really," she conceded, and Nolan laughed. I reached out for the instructions to read them when Kat made an *aw* sort of sound. I looked over her, and she stared at my hand with my wedding band.

"It's so nice to see you wearing that. Liza would be so glad it's no longer sitting in a box," she said.

Liza would be glad—

I froze in place. What had I said about this ring? It was cheap? My heart sank into the pit of my gut, and I felt like the biggest asshole on the planet.

The ring was Crispin's mom's.

"It was so sweet that Crispin asked for it." Kat went on, and I dared a small smile and a nod in her direction.

"It's beautiful." I choked the words out, hoping she didn't hear the self-loathing hidden there.

The table fell into a babble of rules and friendly arguments. I kept the directions in front of my face, pretending to be very enraptured by their contents. I jolted a bit as Crispin moved his hand onto my leg.

"You okay?" he whispered, and I turned my head a bit to meet his face. I shifted my eyes to my ring and then back to him as he followed my gaze. He shook his head, and his expression communicated that I shouldn't worry about what I'd said about *his mom's ring*.

"I didn't know." I raised the directions to cover our faces.

"Nope." His wide grin showed off straight white teeth.

"Why didn't you say anything?"

"What did you want me to say? Excuse me, Maisie, you are insulting my dead mother and father with your commentary about how poor they must have been?"

I winced as I recalled being appalled that The Order would provide me with such a cheap ring. But instead of just apologizing, my whispers got harsher.

"Well, why the hell did you give me your mom's ring in the first place?" I demanded as his eyes went to my hand again, and he opened his mouth to answer.

"We can all hear you." Darcy's voice came as I lowered the directions, reddening. Of course, the table had been able to hear us, and now they were all staring with awkward smiles, except Briar, whose smug smirking made me contemplate our friendship.

"Let's play before Briar gets uninvited to the next game," Nolan said teasingly.

"You don't have the balls to do it, Nolan," she responded, and thankfully, the moment of my embarrassment had passed.

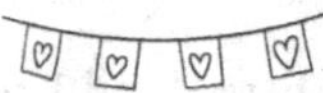

We stood by the car when it was time to go. Kat had just given me a big hug and went to where Crispin, Darcy, and Nolan stood to say her goodbyes to her boys. The Monopoly game hadn't even been close to finished, but we counted up money and property, and Kat had won, which, as I heard it, wasn't that uncommon.

"If you don't like to be hugged, you can just say that." Briar challenged from a couple of feet away.

"Do you mind your own business?" I turned to her.

"You look like you're being stabbed every time. It's painful to watch."

"Some of us care about other people more than we care about our comfort." I folded my arms in protest.

"So you endure out of thoughtfulness? Or is it a selfish need to be liked by everyone?"

"I forgot how insufferable you are."

"Absence makes the heart grow fonder." She pulled out her insulin pump, pressed a button, looked at the screen, and clipped it back on her jeans. "How are you, though? Like for real?"

I admired Briar for a lot of reasons. She was a pain in the ass for almost as many, but she did have some...redeeming qualities. If you squinted and turned your head a bit, you could see them. She genuinely didn't care what most people thought about her. She said what she wanted, when she wanted, and you never had to worry that she was lying to you. So, if she asked how I was, I knew she wasn't just asking to make conversation.

"It started rough, but Crispin and I decided to be friends. Not so awful since then. The blood in the fridge gives me the jeebies a little, but...." I shrugged, not needing to lie or sugarcoat anything for her.

"Just friends? You haven't fallen desperately in love yet?" When the question came out of her mouth, I snorted, but she raised a brow when I looked up into her eyes again.

"You aren't joking?"

"Oh please, you guys were halfway there before you were married. I thought some time in the same sheets may rekindle your romantic rivalry."

"There was no romantic rivalry." I balked.

"Wow, I must have misinterpreted that then." She threw a peace sign up, walking away from me with a grin spread over her stupid face. "Later, Mais."

Eleven

Crispin

"How does it look?" She spun around in her Halloween outfit. I knew she had seen herself in the mirror. She looked incredible, and she knew it.

"You're not getting cold feet about this idea? We can always go as Bonnie and Clyde?" I answered instead of telling her how much I liked the nineties get up on her.

"Hell no." She seemed happier today, and I wanted to know what the secret sauce was and how I could replicate it. But then again, maybe it was selfish of me to wish that she didn't have any hard days.

"Oh really?" I smiled, going over to grab my red button-up and go over my all-black ensemble. "Why the change from *Oh, please, Crispin, be a good boy, and let's not rock the boat.*" I tried to mock her voice in the last bit, and she scoffed at my attempt.

"I'm feeling especially rebellious today. If we have to play by their rules and make it all look real, there is no way to get back at them except by being petty. And I'll tell you what one thing people pleasers like me learn how to do well—petty. This couple's costume is just the thing—not overtly going against their wishes but more of a silent FU. You know?'

"I prefer my middle fingers to be audible." I smirked.

She had a dirty blond wig pinned over her hair, and the synthetic mass was tied back into a low, full bun. She pulled her phone out and walked over to me as we looked at our inspiration photo. What she assured me was an iconic image of Buffy, and Spike came up with him in a red button-up. Sarah Michelle Geller wore a knit skirt with tights and boots, a white shirt, and a fitted leather jacket. I think we replicated it very well. I wasn't wearing a wig but had slicked my hair back.

"I think we nailed it, Mais." I knelt before her like Spike was in the picture, and she chuckled, stuffing the phone into her bag.

We were in another hotel room. This one was big at least and had two separate rooms, so we didn't have to share a bed. This was more of a relief for Maisie than it was for me. I had learned early on that she didn't sleep well. She constantly tossed and turned. It took her a long time to fall asleep, especially if she was having a day where her anxiety was heightened. While she seemed very tired some days, she never slept well enough to be fully refreshed.

"Won't your parents see pictures of us?" I voiced the question I'm sure had occurred to her. "We can't exactly pretend we didn't know that a vampire and slayer costume from *the* vampire show wasn't appropriate."

"No pictures are allowed at the party," she said matter-of-factly. "It's one of the weird rules."

Ah, so this had been a calculated risk on her part.

"But surely someone will tell them about it?" I asked further. I didn't want to set her off, but I also didn't want her to regret it.

"I'm sure they will." That's all she said, and I let it go after that. We left the room and walked out to meet our car service driver in front of the expensive hotel.

"Will you please behave?" she asked as we stood in front of a small mansion of a home.

Why did everyone live in such elaborate houses?

"Why do you always say that?" I asked, reaching up to adjust her blond wig a bit.

In front of the house was a circular driveway packed with high-end cars worth more than my life.

"Because you hardly ever act appropriately." Maisie snorted.

"Should have married someone else. Oh, that's right, you didn't have a choice." I tapped the tip of her nose with my finger as she gave me a withering look. I held up my hands in surrender. "Best behavior, scouts honor, Princess."

She made an unimpressed sound as she pressed the doorbell. We were ushered in by a member of the wait staff who guided us to an outside deck that was bigger than my parents' entire house. Their garden was littered with tables of food and alcohol sprawled out before us, with couples in polished costumes sipping champagne. Luckily, nobody noticed as we came in, and I stood waiting for Maisie's cue on what to do. After all, it was her world, and I was at a loss for what to do next.

We were indeed out of place, as most couples seemed to be dressed as people from history or Disney princes and princesses in dresses so covered in glitz that I was nearly blinded. Even in the dim lighting of the evening, the showiness of it all was unsettling.

"Maisie!" a familiar voice called to us, and we both turned to see the guy Maisie had been talking to at our wedding. He and another man approached; the second looked similar to the first, so I assumed it was his dad.

"Oh, not this asshole," I whispered.

"Best behavior," Maisie reminded me behind a gritted smile, so I smiled, too. I wondered if she was tired of fake smiles and words that meant nothing. "Ajay! Mr. Harrison, it's so nice to see you here."

The older man was dressed as some sort of king I would never be able to get off the top of my head, and Ajay was dressed in a suit of armor.

"Maisie, it was a treat to see you; I didn't get to say congratulations at your wedding. And you as well, Crispin." The older man nodded and put his hand out for me to shake.

"Are you supposed to be in a boyband?" Ajay asked me as I accepted his father's hand.

"Buffy and Spike, from Buffy the Vampire Slayer." Maisie corrected before I could open my mouth and say something rude.

"Oh," the older man said, obviously a bit shocked. "How very clever. I must tell Celia you are here; she's dying to see you." He excused himself, so we were alone with a man who wouldn't stop staring at my wife like she belonged to him. I tried very hard to ignore it.

"Where is the lucky damsel in distress to your chivalrous knight?" I asked instead, rather proud of myself that it only came out slightly mocking.

"Hailee Brawn is the Guinevere to my Lancelot," he explained like I was a child, and he would get crayons out to draw a diagram for me in a moment.

"Perhaps she's run off the nunnery then," I said, and it was his turn to look confused as I turned to Maisie. "I am going to grab something to eat. Do you want anything?"

"No, you go ahead. I'll be down by the pool house. I see my friend Taylor."

I wanted to grab her and kiss her—not to mark my territory—*well, yes, okay to mark my territory*. She didn't belong to me, but I didn't like this guy looking at her like he was just waiting for me to walk away to make his move. But I touched the small of her back as I passed and told her I'd find her in a few minutes.

I stepped to the nearest food table and took a few calming breaths. I didn't even turn around to see if she was still talking to him. I didn't want to know.

"Crispin!" a voice called, and I looked up to see my cousin's girlfriend, Fern, waving and walking toward me.

"Oh hey," I smiled, still loading my plate with fruit, meat, and cheese. Her hair had changed from the foxlike colors it had been at our wedding, and now it was a striking icy blond that was very near white. "Is Jaggar here?" I half attempted to scan the crowd for him, not looking but more to seem like I cared.

"Yeah, of course! It's one of the parties of the year."

"So I hear."

"What are your and Maisie's costumes?" she asked, her voice chipper and light.

"It's a vampire and slayer couple from a TV show," I explained because, admittedly, I knew very little of Buffy the Vampire Slayer. I had watched a few rerun episodes, but Maisie was the super fan. Apparently, she had fantasies about being Buffy when she was younger, which was slightly offensive if I thought about it too hard.

"Immaculate," she giggled.

"Crispin, it's good to see you." A voice came from behind me, and I frowned down at the plate of food.

Kirk Hillbrand.

My grandfather, my mother's father, was standing behind me. I knew the calm and collected cadence of his voice, though I had only heard it a handful of times.

"Hello." I turned and did my best to mimic a Maisie smile.

I just returned his greeting instead of greeting him by his name, mostly because I was unsure what to call him. Grandfather felt awkward and inappropriate, but Kirk also felt uncomfortable. Then again, Mr. Hillbrand felt like I was still in high school addressing a teacher, so my hello would have to suffice.

He was a tall, stately man, slender, with a full head of white hair and blue eyes that matched mine. I hated him for that. I didn't want to have the same eyes as a man who never cared to know me. Who gave up on any kind of relationship as soon as he didn't get his way. I'd rather have eyes like Nolan Booker. Nolan

Booker taught me how to shovel snow, tie a tie, and be a good friend. I wanted eyes like Kat Booker, who taught me how to respect a woman, how to drive, and how to make a decent cup of coffee.

Instead, I stared into the eyes of a man who had abandoned my mother because she fell in love with the wrong person— and my gaze was the same as his.

"It's nice to see you. You and your bride look...unique this evening," he said awkwardly, and I watched as Fern backed away slowly from us.

Smart.

"Thank you...sir," I said the last part almost like a question.

"Have you been enjoying your travels?" He pressed on.

"I suppose it's nice to see other things besides Ironside." I shuffled my feet back and forth.

"Your mother loved to travel." He smiled a bit then, and I almost felt bad for him. He had lost his daughter, after all.

"Were my parents killed by vampire hunters?" I asked bluntly. I felt bad for springing the question on him, but you could often get a more honest answer that way, and since nobody seemed to want to tell me exactly what happened, this seemed a good opportunity. I watched the words assault him as he flinched. He took a minute of silence as we stared at each other with the same eyes.

"Yes, by a band of hunters who held to the old ways—men who thought they could get to me by killing her."

No wonder my parents had never told me. My vision swam as I fought the urge to vomit.

"Alright. Thanks for being honest." I managed to choke out.

"I feel I owe you more than that, but...." His voice was strained as I struggled to control my emotions. I could see now he was vulnerable. Water collected at the corners of his eyes, but I couldn't think about his loss just then.

My loss was strange. Birth parents I didn't remember lost to a group of murderers who couldn't let go of a broken system. The people who raised me lost their best friends and had to take on a child that wasn't theirs. Now, I was married to someone who belonged to the same group, maybe a more progressive version, but Maisie's father had made it clear that he was still wary of me. The distrust between hunters and vampires seemed too large to bridge at that moment.

I hated this party.

My grandfather dismissed himself with some halfhearted mumble about making the rounds, and I turned back to the table to see if there was some sort of alcohol.

Surely that would help, right?

"Your grandfather is such a respectable man."

I groaned and tried to ignore the voice of Maisie's number-one fan club member. It was blow after blow, and I wasn't sure how much more I could handle. A champagne fountain was at the end of the table, and I walked over to it, trying to understand where I was supposed to take a glass from. From the top? Was it just for decoration?

"Your costume choice is funny," Ajay went on, not taking the hint that I was ignoring him.

"Listen, dude. I don't want to talk to you. I'm not sure why you are over here," I said honestly, scowling at the champagne fountain, unable to ascertain how to get a glass without massive damage.

"Are you intimidated by me?" he asked, and I heard the smugness in his voice.

I opened my mouth to say something but thought better and closed it before I turned. "Maybe. I don't really feel like giving you the time necessary to sort it out. I don't like you. I don't like how you look at Maisie. Maybe it's insecurity—I can't be sure. What I am sure of is that I want you to go somewhere else and leave me alone." The answer my grandfather gave me was taking up too much room in my chest at that moment to deal with this.

"Oh, but we have so much to talk about."

"I can't imagine we do." I controlled my breathing and my fangs, which threatened to pop out at the mere proximity of this jerk.

"Sure, we do, buddy." He leaned forward and grabbed my shoulder, shaking me as if we were old pals.

Keep it together, Crispin.

"You and I are the only men in the world who have slept with your beautiful bride after all." He droned on, and his voice became a sort of underwater sound as anger flooded through me, and my hands were clenched at my sides. My eyes flicked up and across the party's expense until they found Maisie. An older woman was talking to her, but she was looking directly at me, shaking her head.

"Honestly, has she loosened up any over the years? She was so uptight. But that's my Maisie, always in control of her emotions. Though I suppose if you're sleeping with a vampire, relaxing would be a challenge." The idiot prattled on like I wasn't about to rip his throat out for calling Maisie his.

What lurked in the darker part of me was closer to taking control. The shadow of who I was did not like him calling her *My Maisie*. I knew he was trying to goad me, and I knew I should just walk away. I tried to channel my inner Darcy. He was the good one, the better one....

"Well, I guess it doesn't matter. When she comes to her senses, I'll always be there for her."

I punched him square in the face and smiled a little when I heard the crack of cartilage. I held back a little, but not much.

Ajay hollered, holding his face as blood poured from his nose. I ensured my fangs weren't out, and I stepped forward, keeping my voice even. "Can I get you some ice for that?"

Ajay looked at me like I was some sort of psycho, but eventually, I looked around to meet the eyes of everyone who was now staring at us, passing judgment.

The bastard vampire prince was causing trouble at such a lovely party. The vampire was out of control, just like we always were, and that's what they would always see. Again, I hadn't given them anything but what they expected.

I met Maisie's gaze again. She stared at me, not angrily, but with a terrible disappointment that caused me to flinch away from her. I watched her as she turned to leave as Ajay flew at me and knocked me back into the pristine champagne fountain.

Twelve

Maisie

My hands shakily pulled a cigarette from the pack as I stood on the street in front of the house. I swallowed my emotions and stuffed them away as fast as they bubbled out. I had my meds in my purse just in case I needed them, but I was trying not to need them.

Mad at Crispin was an understatement. I left him alone for five seconds, and he punched someone. Not just anyone, either, Ajay. Though I knew Ajay had sought Crispin out, most likely to get under his skin. Couldn't Crispin just walk away? Would I have to be worried for the rest of our five years together that he would explode at any sign of conflict? My heart rate increased, my throat grew tight, and the cigarette hung loosely in my fingers at my side.

Voices pulled me out of the numbing spiral my brain had been about to take. I looked nervously to my left to see Jaggar and Fern laughing with each other as they walked to a car. I quickly tried to look like I was just out taking a smoke break. Everyone at the party had seen what happened, and I'm sure if they saw me, they would assume I was upset.

Jaggar looked a lot like Crispin, with more of a California vibe about him, and Fern was an effortless, cool girl. She was the kind who would look good if she rolled out of bed in an oversized t-shirt with mussed hair. Jaggar was wearing all black and some pirate-esque boots, and Fern was wearing a long, flowing red dress with billowing sleeves and a sort of golden sash tied around her waist. I only knew who they were because Jaggar wore a black mask.

They did, in fact, notice me and waved. I groaned quietly but nodded at them in greeting. They made their way over to me, which was even worse.

"Princess Bride," I acknowledged as they got closer so they didn't have to break any awkward greeting. "Very cool."

"See, Babe, I told you, the girls who get it get it." She bumped him, and he rolled his eyes at her, but in an affectionate way that reminded me too much of my husband.

"You bouncing?" Jaggar asked, and I nodded, but then I had an idea.

"You guys know any good clubs around here?"

"Of course! We live thirty minutes away." Fern volunteered, and I sighed, relieved.

I wasn't going back to the hotel to wallow. If I took my wig off, fixed my hair, and removed the jacket, I think the outfit could pass as trendy club wear. *Maybe. I didn't really know.*

"Partake is a good one, isn't it?" Jaggar asked Fern as she looked up at him thoughtfully.

"Yeah, it's not too wild," she agreed. "But they won't let you in without a pass. I think I have one." She rummaged around in her purse.

"Oh no, that's okay," I assured not wanting her to go to trouble.

"No worries, they expire in forty-eight hours anyway and I won't be able to use it." She found it finally and waved it in the air triumphantly. "Ticketed clubs are safer around here anyway."

"Only if you're sure." She handed it over with a kind smile, and I tucked it in my bag. Without any other questions, I typed in the address from Google on my phone and called myself an Uber. The pictures looked nice enough, and I wanted to get out of there, but I also didn't want to be sitting around whenever Crispin decided to come back to the hotel.

"That was a crazy time," Fern said sympathetically.

"Is Crispin okay?" I asked, looking over at them. I had watched Ajay push him into the champagne, but I still left without checking on either of them.

"Yeah, he's right; he's just getting cleaned up. I think he got a cut, but he'll be healed soon, don't worry," Jaggar assured me, and I nodded. "The other guy, however— double black eyes if I'm any sort of judge."

"At least this year wasn't so boring." Fern chimed in.

The conversation went quiet after that. I finished the cigarette in my hand and kept looking down as the Uber slowly approached.

"You guys don't have to wait with me. Go back and enjoy the party."

"Oh, we don't mind. At least we know you're safe," Fern assured.

"Then I can at least tell my cousin we made sure you got in your car." Jaggar agreed. "He's a hothead, but he cares about you."

I didn't want to think about that. I could control my emotions more if they were just anger.

"It's the moon eyes that give it away." Fern agreed, and I wanted to beg them to stop. I knew they were trying to help, but I didn't want to think about anything except that I needed Crispin to act like a decent human. Tonight, he had acted like a vampire.

The thought shook me, and I chastised myself. Vampirism wasn't an attitude or a behavior. Vampires were people with temperaments as diverse as anyone else. I was no better than my father. Guilt added to the other litany of emotions.

Fern smoked another cigarette with me until the car showed up. She and Jaggar talked about their recent trip to the Redwoods and its unique nature. I listened and nodded, asking a polite question from time to time, but they were kind enough to carry the conversation for me. Fern hugged me tightly before I got into the car, and I didn't try to shrug her off before they waved me off.

I greeted the driver but then got to work deconstructing my costume. Once happy with the results, I leaned back into the leather seat and looked out the window as we passed into the city. My phone pinged several times, and on inspection, it was Crispin asking where I had gone.

I shoved the phone back into my purse, ignoring him.

The music was pulsing perfectly with the stone of the lights. The club was like something out of a movie, which is what the idea of a nightclub might be. It was all sexy men and women whispering at open tables and dancing on the three dance floors available while a DJ mixed music on a large platform off to the left. Despite the odd entrance down an alley, the guy at the door was serious about the ticket that Fern had given me. However, he seemed happy enough to let me in once I handed it to him.

I walked up to the main bar and sat on one of the only available stools.

"What will it be, gorgeous?" the bartender asked. He was a handsome man with deep brown skin and hair styled in meticulous braids. His smile was kind, and he seemed patient enough to wait for me to answer.

"Gin and Tonic." I tried to sound sure, but he must have sensed a hesitation in my voice. The only alcohol I really drank were hard lemonades my mom's sister brought over when she visited. But that seemed juvenile to order, so I stuck with something I'd seen in movies. The bartender's mouth tilted up in a half smile.

"I told the boys up front to stop letting you young ones in." He turned and poured something up that I couldn't see.

He was dressed in a black turtleneck and dark wash jeans, like the other bartenders around him. The girls who served drinks to the tables wore white turtlenecks instead.

"Tonic and lime." He pushed it across the bar. "Drink it, take a good look around, and then get your skinny behind out of here. You are too young to be a partaken. My name's Andrew. If you need anything or if trouble finds you in here."

I passed him my credit card over the counter, and he waved it away before walking over to help someone else. I sipped the bitter soda laced with lime, feeling thoroughly chastised by Andrew, who had seen me for what I was: An insecure, anxiety-ridden nineteen-year-old who didn't even know how to order a drink properly. Why the hell was I even here? To piss Crispin off? To piss my parents off, who would never even know I was here?

FU, Mom, and Dad. I'm in a nightclub in a different city, drinking terrible lime soda. I'm really sticking it to you, aren't I?

My anxiety had settled a little bit. It was the excess noise and movement around me. There was so much to focus on that I couldn't internalize anything. I pushed the half-drunk glass away from me and stood up. I was going home and taking a bath, and then I'd order some damn food. Whatever food I wanted.

I waved to Andrew, hoping he could see the thanks in my eyes as he nodded and waved back. I walked around the dance floor in the middle of the place. Someone dancing got a little too close to me, and in an attempt not to bump into them, I hit the edge of a table with my thigh.

"Oh gosh, I'm so sorry," I said to the two guys and the girl who sat on the round bench behind it.

The girl was older than me, maybe in her mid-twenties, and the guys looked around the same age, maybe older. One was pale with freckles and red hair and wore a loose bun on the back of his head. The other two had olive skin and darker brown hair. Based on their coloring and facial features, they were siblings.

"No trouble at all. Is your leg okay?" The dark-haired man spoke. His grin was goofy and lopsided.

"Oh yes, I'm fine."

"I'm Ollie!" The man stood up and leaned over the table a little to offer me his hand, which I took. "This is Sylvia and Kenny." They both waved to me with their own grins.

"Nice to meet you, but I was just leaving."

"Oh, what a tragedy that would be!" Kenny said. We've just ordered a round of Partake lemon drop shots; we can add one more if you like." His accent, which I thought may have been midwestern, gave him a homey and charming quality.

I was going to take a car home anyway. What would one drink hurt before I went to my bath and delivered food?

"Sure," I shrugged, and Ollie moved over so I could sit with them.

"Where are you all from?" I asked as they flagged a waitstaff member and ordered one more drink for me.

"Kenny is from Ohio, and Sylvia and I are from Minnesota."

We all talked briefly as they told me about their trip across the country. They had rented an RV after graduating and were taking six months to see it all.

When the waitress returned, she put a tall shot glass before everyone.

"To our new friend!" Ollie said, holding up his glass before we all drank. After that one, they ordered more, and I opened my purse to see five missed calls and two texts from Crispin. I gritted my teeth, the earlier anger fresh in my mind, as I stuffed it back and closed my purse.

Thirteen

Crispin

"You ever been to a vampire club?" I asked, panic layered in my voice over the phone from where I sat in the back of the vehicle. Luckily, the driver had a divider between me and him, and I had raised it before calling my brother.

"Crispin, this is your eighteen-year-old brother— Darcy? Remember?"

"Right, sorry."

"It's okay, man. What happened?" Darcy's voice was groggy. I'd definitely woken him up.

"I did something to piss Maisie off, and she left this fancy party we were at."

I thought she had just gone out to smoke, but when I went out to find her, my cousin and his girlfriend said she had called an Uber and left. Fern had said they didn't know where she had gone. I'd called her like a million times. I finally called Trudy, and she sent me her location after a fair amount of explaining and evading.

I breathed the whole story out to Darcy in what seemed like one breath. I felt like a piece of shit. I shouldn't have punched that guy, Ajay, even if he was an asshole. I told Maisie I would behave, and at the first sign of Douche Canoe, I had blown my top.

"Why would she go to a vampire club?" Darcy questioned.

"Because she's a moron," I answered, my fingers gripping my cell phone tighter.

"How would she even know where to find one? How would she get in? They normally have a pretty extensive selection process, don't they?"

"I don't know, Darcy; how would I know?"

"Alright, alright." He yawned. "Well, you have her location. She probably just went to blow off a little steam, and she accidentally hit a blood club."

"You sound very nonchalant for someone who knows what happens to humans in these places. Not to mention, if she gets bit and The Guild finds out, it will be a massive problem."

"Let's hope they don't. Let's also hope she doesn't get bit."

I tried to push the idea of some random vampire biting Maisie. It bothered me for more than one reason, but I wasn't going to think about it. It was my fault she had left— I knew that. It would be partially my fault if she got bit. But why the hell would she go to a vampire club? Maybe Darcy was right, and she had just picked one at random.

"It'll be okay." Darcy's reassurance normally helped me, but I was still worked up.

"I don't want to do this anymore," I said instead, feeling the uncomfortable weight of the words on my chest.

"I know, Dude."

"I don't belong around these people. I obviously can't handle it. You would be so much better at this."

"I don't think I would."

"What are you talking about? You would be exactly what these people want. You're nice and good, and I'm...obviously a fucking mess."

"First of all, I'm not sure these people need *nice*, and I'm not good. Do you have a problem controlling your anger? Sure, you need to work on that, but do you know what I have a problem with? People pleasing. I always want everyone to be happy, and that's worse at times. I'm pretty sure this whole thing needs a little shake, Crispin, and I'm not the guy that shakes things up—you are. Maisie needs someone who will stick up for her, not someone who is trying to make peace with everyone."

I couldn't say anything because the weight in my chest had moved to my throat, and I was afraid if any words came out, they would be acomnpanied by weeping. I would not bawl in the back of this car like a child.

"I'm not the good one. You always say shit like that, and it's dumb. Maybe less punching, but you should just still be you. If the system is going to change, we need a changer. You're a changer."

"Alright, alright, okay," I said, swallowing the lump.

"Also, if that guy said that stuff about Briar, I would have a hard time controlling myself. Maybe try an open-palm slap next time. It's more dramatic."

"I'll try and remember that." I smiled a little. "I'm about to pull up now."

"Text me when you find her."

"Okay, I will."

"Love you."

"Love you."

The driver agreed to keep the car running, and when the bouncer in the front tried to give me crap about the car being parked there, I became a version of my father. Sometimes, a situation calls for controlled rage. I could use it as a tool instead of it using me. *How many times had he tried to tell me that?*

"Are you aware that you've let an underage human in there?" He hesitated as I forged on. "And not only that; she's a hunter."

His eyes widened, and at least that shut him up. He was a big guy, much bigger and broader than me. I supposed you wanted the front guys at a club to be intimidating, and this guy was it.

"She's about this tall, curly brown hair, pretty face," I said, holding my hand out, and he nodded slightly. "She's also a hunter, so if she gets bit in there—."

"Get her out of the club," he said, speaking into his walkie a color code that made no sense to me.

"I plan to."

I pushed past him and into the noisy place. I shut my eyes against the cacophony of music and talking, wondering how vampires sat here dancing and feeding. I was having trouble concentrating at all. I knew that my senses were heightened because I was in my young adult years. I was stronger but also more responsive to light and sounds.

This situation reminded me too much of when Adam and Morgan Pope turned the fire alarm on, and Maisie went missing.

Maybe that's why I felt so nervous. I walked around a long time before I ended up at one of the bars and caught the bartender's attention.

"You looking for someone?" he asked, shaking something all the while.

"Yeah, short woman with dark curly hair." I felt like I had to yell over the noise, though I didn't.

"Human?" he asked, knowing in his eyes.

"Hunter," I countered.

"Fuck." He poured his drink and walked it to the waiting patron before returning to me. "She was at the bar probably Forty-ish minutes ago. I told her to go home. Hold on." I stood there as he walked to the end of the counter and talked to a girl serving drinks. She blanched a little at whatever he said and pointed in a general direction. Before the guy could return, I was headed to where she had pointed.

I wove through people dancing and brushed off rogue hands that reached for me. The music crashed over me like waves threatening to drown, but keeping my eyes on my destination, I kept calm. Taking several deep breaths, my eyes grazed over several open tables.

There, at a table with a few other people, sat Maisie. She smiled and talked without caring about controlling her expressions. I got myself in check before I approached them. My anger had run away with me once tonight already. No reason to let it again.

"Maisie," I said as I approached, and her eyes met mine. Before, she looked so happy, but now she grimaced.

Oof.

"How did you find me?" she asked, and I saw the posture of the others around her go slightly rigid. Her words were blurred together like cursive, and she had a high blush on her cheeks.

"Trudy," I explained. "We need to go home, Mais." I kept my voice gentle and calm because I knew what this could look like.

"You know this guy, Maisie?" A redhead guy asked her, and I begged her with my eyes not to make a scene.

"He's my husband." She giggled after she said it like it was the best joke she'd ever made.

"Husband?" The girl in the group asked, staring directly at me. "She's a human."

It was more an accusation than anything. Human and vampire marriages were looked down upon, even in circles where vampires used humans as blood bags. The stigma was lessening, but the assumption was that the human was addicted to the bite of their partner, and that's why they stayed.

"She is." I nodded. "Maisie, you don't want to be here."

"Yes, I do. These are my new friends." She gestured around, her head bobbing around to the music.

I leaned over the table so that my words wouldn't carry to any other patrons. "Your friends got you drunk and are planning on drinking your blood. Maisie, this is a vampire bar. You cannot be here."

"Bro, she can if she wants." The brown-haired man argued with me as he put his arm around her shoulders. Maisie looked uncomfortable at the contact, and I worked my jaw back and forth. I didn't have anything against him. I tried hard not to judge those who indulged in this lifestyle. I didn't like the idea, and I thought it was preying on human weakness, but I tried not to assume every vampire who blood flashed was a bad person.

"Listen, man, she's not even old enough to be here; she's nineteen years old. Also, she's a hunter."

Maisie glared at me, but the others froze in place.

"Did you bite her?" I asked, looking over Maisie, who, while drunk off her ass, didn't seem otherwise harmed.

"You're lying," the girl accused again, and I leveled her with a glare.

"Check the back of her neck. She's got the mark. I'm not here to cause trouble. However, if you don't let her go, you'll have more than a pissed-off husband to deal with. The Guild and The Order will be all over your asses."

"Ollie." The girl said as she reached over and lifted up Maisie's short hair. Maisie batted her hand away.

"I'll go," my wife said. They didn't protest, and the red-haired man looked a little relieved. Ollie exited the booth so Maisie could slide out. She did so rather ungracefully, nearly falling over.

"We didn't know." Ollie defended with a wince in his words.

"The club is supposed to check the age of entrants, but maybe before you put your fangs into anyone, you should double-check," I hissed at him. My mind kept wondering if I had been any later and this man had drunk from Maisie. Jealousy and rage threatened to color my vision.

It didn't happen. I reminded myself.

"I'd step back, or he'll break your nose," Maisie slurred, and I rolled my eyes. Why did I have a feeling this wasn't the last time I was going to hear about this?

I didn't have time to argue with her or baby her out the front door, so I just picked her up instead.

"Put me down," she said, pushing her arms against my chest.

Maisie was athletic, and the muscles in her arms pushed against me, but I was stronger, and she was drunk. While I may have been sturdier than most humans, that didn't mean carrying a whole-ass person was easy.

"Have a good evening," I said by way of goodbye as the three stared at us and then at each other as if wondering if they should try to stop me. Thankfully, they didn't.

Maisie got herself into the car and slid all the way over so that she was the furthest away from me that she could be. The driver started the trip back to our hotel, and a strange silence fell between us. She wasn't tapping or fidgeting so it was hard for me to tell if she was alright or...not. I took several steadying breaths, wondering how I apologized for my behavior at the party. How many times could you apologize for the same thing before it didn't mean anything? Even in the club, part of me had been more worried about her being bitten than if she was okay. This whole thing was a mess.

"I didn't know," she said, breaking the silence first. "About the club, I didn't know. I'm stupid, but not that stupid."

I just nodded as she leaned her head back and rolled down the car window.

"I'm going to be sick."

Fourteen

Maisie

I'd made it to the hotel room before I'd vomited. The walls spun, and my head was throbbing. Four shots and half a beer were too much for someone who had only partaken in light vodka lemonades. My stomach rioted against me as I groaned into the toilet bowl.

I was vaguely aware of Crispin's presence, but I couldn't be bothered with him then. I had gone to a vampire bar, drank too much, and had almost been bitten by the people who bought me the drinks. There were three of them; had they all planned to drink from me? I shivered as my hand went to my throat. If Crispin hadn't come....

I got sick again and threw up everything else in my stomach into the toilet and then dry heaved for a minute longer. When I pulled up, I smelled vomit and reached to feel that I had gotten some in my hair.

"Aw, yuck," I grumbled, looking over to the shower. It seemed a mile away as I crawled on my hands and knees toward it. I sat before it, stripping down to my pink lacy bralette and pink underwear. I opened the glass door and crawled inside.

I stared helplessly at the handle to turn on the water, which I couldn't reach from where I was. *Maybe I would just sleep here—*With throw-up in my hair as the tiles spun, and I had to keep closing my eyes to keep from feeling nauseous.

"Whatcha doing?" Crispin's voice came to me, but I couldn't bear to open my eyes to find him.

"I have vomit in my hair," I lamented, and I heard him draw nearer.

"Ah." It was more a sound than a response. "Want me to turn the water on?"

I nodded, and as I heard him fiddle with the nozzle, I braced myself for the first shock of cold water. It never came. I opened my eyes enough to see he had pointed the head away from me and had his fingers in the stream to feel the water temperature. When he decided it was warm enough, he turned it to hit my knees, which were pulled up to my chest.

I looked up at the shampoo bottles on a lower ledge, but they were still too far away to think about climbing. It might as well have been Jobs Peak right then. Crispin reached across, the water trailing down his arm and onto his white tank top, which he had worn under his button-up.

"Ah, screw it." He stepped into the shower and closed the door behind him. Panic gripped me as he grabbed the shampoo bottles and sat on the tiles before me. His hair and shirt were soaked. His pants would be next.

"What?" I managed to get out.

"You can't even move. You think you're going to wash your hair? Lean forward," he commanded, and so without rebuttal or complaint, I did.

He worked his fingers through my hair, first thoroughly soaking my locks as I sat there, enjoying the feeling of the water washing over us. Eventually, I heard him open my shampoo, and with a gentleness I was surprised by, he pushed my head up and started working the soap through my hair.

"Listen, Mais, I'm sorry about tonight."

Oh no, you idiot, don't apologize. I started crying. He seemed awkwardly silent, but he didn't tell me not to cry.

"I'm not upset about you." I managed to sniffle. "Well, not just you."

"What a relief. You shampoo once or twice?"

"Once."

"Conditioner it is." He worked his hands delicately through my curls, wrapping his finger around a few of them and smiling absently. His touch cleaved my chest open, and warmth flooded me. I then realized I liked him washing my hair. His calm movements and warmth soothed me, so I wanted to lean into him instead of pull away.

"Listen, we are going to get this right, okay? I'm obviously not the best at... rich people. But I can do better, and we can communicate more. So if your evil ex comes around, I can say excuse me, gorgeous wife, I think it is time for me to go drown in the pool."

I shook with laughter, which was strange as I knew I still had tears on my face.

"You think I'm gorgeous?" I closed my eyes as he washed the conditioner out, not wanting him to finish.

"Yes," he said so quietly that the water may as well have washed it away. But the smile that graced my face was all balmy and light.

"A pain in the ass though, like really, Pope." He took my chin in his hand, tilting my head up. He made a few passes at what I assumed was my running mascara with his thumbs. "You look crazy right now. Like the Joker or something."

"Wow, thanks." *Please don't kiss me. Not right now. Not with a throw-up mouth.*

The internal words intruded unwanted. And I wondered if that was my only qualm with him kissing me. Did I want him to kiss me? My head swam with conflicting answers that I couldn't make sense of.

"You want me to grab you some clothes?" I was startled back to him by the question, and I hoped the hot water would cover my flushed face.

"Pink satin pajamas with clouds on them." My most comfortable and favorite pair.

He got out, leaving me with just warm water. After a couple of minutes, I slid up the side of the shower and washed myself the best I could. Leaving my bra and underwear in the shower, I stepped out and trampled into the water piles Crispin had left behind. I wrapped myself in a towel and realized he had already set my pajamas on the counter.

I was slow as a slug with a walker as I dried off and slathered some body oil that smelled like vanilla and lemon. If I went to bed without wrapping my hair, it would be out of control tomorrow, but I didn't care about that just then. I gently towel-dried it, put some oil in it, and hoped for the best because that was all that would happen. I cleaned my face, removed the joker makeup, and moisturized. I brushed my teeth and said my goodbyes to my contaminated toothbrush before throwing it in the trash.

I felt like a better version of myself; that version had still been clocked with an anvil, but at least her teeth were brushed. When I entered the hallway and my bedroom, I saw a cup of tea on the nightstand beside my bed.

"I thought we could watch something unless you're tired," Crispin said behind me, and I slipped beneath the heavenly hotel bedding.

"Thanks for the tea and washing my hair." I smiled at him almost shyly. He leaned against the doorframe in salmon sweatpants with our high school logo on the side.

"Sure, didn't know if you could keep anything down, and it's also hotel tea, but...." He shrugged.

"Let's watch something on this TV. I'm too lazy to move." I snuggled into the bed and sipped the tea. It was disgusting.

Crispin grabbed the remote and sat beside me atop the comforter as he flipped through channels. The movie Blast from the Past came on, and I made him stop and watch it even though it was halfway over.

"I feel like I want to watch from the beginning," he grumbled.

"Be quiet. Your gorgeous wife has spoken." I waved him off.

"Oh my goodness, you've let that go to your head." But he settled in and watched the rest of the movie with me.

I was vaguely aware of him taking the tea mug out of my hands and setting it on the nightstand. I opened my eyes to see the credits rolling. Crispin turned the TV and the lights off as I snuggled under the blankets, sleep sounding delightful to my slightly throbbing head.

Crispin walked to the door.

"Hey, Crispin," I called out. The words were out before I could stop and weigh what they would cost me.

"Hm?" He turned back slightly, his face mostly hidden in the dark.

"Would you...maybe...." *Oh*, these words weren't coming out as easily as the first ones. He just stood waiting for me to speak. "Will you stay with me? In here?"

"Oh," he said, and I heard the hesitation in his voice which made me cringe. "I can do that," he said finally, and I released a quiet breath. He left momentarily and returned with a glass of water for his side of the bed. He had put on a tank top, and I almost made fun of him. We shared a bed on our honeymoon, and he was much less dressed then. Was this different? More significant than before?

He slid under the covers and lay there stiff for a few minutes.

"Can I ask you another favor?" I asked, though my eyelids drifted close.

"Sure."

"Would you come like...hold me?"

"Like cuddle you?" I heard the smirk that made me want to slap him.

"Yeah, listen." I groaned, knowing how it sounded and hating that I was coming off as needy. It didn't bother me as much as usual, but I knew he could use this against me later. "I'm not great with physical affection...."

"I've noticed," he interrupted, and I sighed.

"Yeah, well, in the shower, I didn't like hate you touching me–my head," I corrected quickly, but he didn't say anything. "So I thought maybe...."

Instead of answering, he slid over and drew me against the front of him so he was spooning me. One of his arms reached under my pillow, and one came around my midsection. I don't know what I had been expecting, but it was very close, and almost every part of me touched some of him.

I let his weight sit with me momentarily before I relaxed into him. It was just like earlier. His encasing me didn't feel stuffy or cloying. It felt comforting and warm.

"So?" he inquired curiously.

"Good."

"Okay then, Princess."

When had *Princess* stopped sounding like he was mocking me?

Fifteen

Crispin

Maisie hadn't said a word the whole plane ride back home. To be fair, she had slept a fair amount and worn headphones the rest of the time.

I tried not to laugh at her in her hungover state.

I tried even harder not to think of how I had awoken to her pressed into the back of me, her deep breaths on my neck, and her hand slung low on my waist. I extracted myself, showered, and put on coffee for us to make our mid-morning flight. She had not been happy when I had shaken her awake.

Now, we sat at the luggage carousel at the airport nearest our house. She dressed in baggy black Fila sweats, but the logo was pink, so it was about as goth as she got. Her sunglasses were dark, large, and tinted. Her hair was untamed and wild, the curls going wherever they wanted. I wanted to run my hands through it like I had yesterday, but it seemed inappropriate now.

"I need pads and a new toothbrush," she grumbled as I rolled our luggage across the parking lot. Hers was designer in her preferred color, and mine was a floral old lady suitcase my mother had given me. I'm pretty sure it belonged to her mom before her.

"Okay, we can stop at the store." We got to my truck, and I slid the luggage into the back.

"You want food?" I asked.

"Maybe like a greasy fast-food hamburger," she suggested, shrinking in her seat. "And a Diet Coke."

I found the nearest drive-thru and smiled as she inhaled a few french fries. I pulled into a store parking lot, and she glared at the front entrance.

"I'll just go in and be right back." I grabbed my phone and wallet.

"You're going to get me pads and a toothbrush?" she asked incredulously.

"Yes?" I questioned, opening the door.

"How will you know which ones?" She took a big bite of her burger and talked around the mouthful.

"Well, there's this cool thing called texting, and if you message me the name or a picture, I'm sure I can figure it out from there."

"Okay, asshole, I got it." She waved me out, and I entered the store, grabbing one of those odd handheld baskets. I took my phone out and dialed Jessica's number. I offered to come inside alone for two reasons: Maisie looked like she didn't want to come in, and I didn't want her to know I was going to call Jessica.

"Mr. Booker." The woman's tone was clipped as soon as she picked up.

"Jessica," I repeated as I located the toothbrush aisle while I waited for Maisie's text.

"If you are calling to apologize about your behavior...."

"Do you think I would call to apologize to you?" I interrupted her and then bit my tongue, remembering I was trying to be better. "I mean, no, Jessica, that is not why I'm calling."

"Unsurprising," she said while waiting for why I *had* called.

I crouched in the empty aisle with my little blue basket and phone to my ear, looking at the toothbrush options.

"There's a club called Partake near where we were at that party yesterday."

"A club?" I could hear the exasperation in her voice.

"A flash blood club," I said a little quieter as she went silent on the other line. I selected a child toothbrush with a pony, as it was the only one with extra-soft bristles. "Well, anyway, I don't want to get into it, but they are letting underage and unwitting humans in, apparently."

"How do you know that?" she asked after a bit of silence.

"Just do."

"Crispin, I hope I do not have to tell you how inappropriate it would be for you to go to a club of that kind. You are the public face of The Order and The Guild right now."

"Is it illegal?"

"No," she ground out, her voice tight. Her dislike for me was more evident than ever.

"Maybe it should be." I sighed. "No, Jessica, I was not there to participate in club activities, but I was there."

"Is Maisie fine?" her voice was softer now that she was talking about my human wife.

"She is."

"Was she...." She hesitated on the edge of the question.

"No, but she could have been."

My phone pinged, and as I pulled the phone away from my ear, I saw the packages of pads and tampons Maisie wanted me to get.

"I'll take care of it, Mr. Booker."

"I know you will; that's why I called you and not The Order." I hung up the phone and slid it into my pocket as I located the feminine product aisle.

I figured I could grab some things for our house fridge while I was there. I snagged some cream for coffee and some frozen fruit for the smoothies Maisie liked to make in the mornings. I scanned the chocolate aisle and picked a few bars out for her. I had a few other ingredients for easy lunches and dinners. My basket was overflowing, and then I had an idea. I dragged my haul to the craft section and grabbed a large science board, markers, and embroidery thread.

I should have grabbed a rolling cart, and I looked ridiculous trying to balance everything while making my way up to self-checkout.

"What the heck did you get?" Maisie asked, looking at the stuff I had hauled into the backseat.

"How does pizza and crafts later this evening sound?" I asked, getting into the driver's seat.

"Honestly, great." She popped one of the last french fries into her mouth.

"What is this going to be exactly?" Maisie asked, eyeing the open pizza boxes.

When we got home, I got her to go to the gym with me, and now she stared over our dining table in her workout clothes.

"Okay, so my idea is to map out what we have to attend until the spring and connect families together so we will know who people are."

"This will look like a crime board." She picked up a blue marker. I had accidentally grabbed scented markers, and she opened the cap and sniffed it, making a face.

"I hope so." I got to work marking out events based on Jessica's list, which she had emailed us. It detailed appearances for the next few months. Maisie got to work printing pictures of people off on the printer that The Guild and The Order had provided us on a desk in the corner. We ended up taking two other pieces of paper and making family trees of her family and mine, and then any events that were directly related to them got tied with the pink embroidery thread.

We admired our handiwork, which did, in fact, look like a crime board.

"Is it still okay for us to meet Erik and Trudy tomorrow for breakfast?" Maisie asked, opening her phone to text her best friend.

"Of course, it's been too long since we've seen them," I answered absently. "How are you explaining all the traveling to Trudy?"

"How are you explaining it to Erik?" she countered.

"He's never asked. But I'm sure he's asked Trudy if she knows." I shrugged. When I texted Erik a couple of times just to touch base, he gave me updates on how his internship at the Carbon Fiber shop was going and how Trudy thought he should sign up to coach an elementary basketball team. Besides that, we hadn't connected in a while, and it would be good to see him.

"I told her I'm doing some interning for my dad."

"Smart." I nodded and headed to get the tacky wall strips to display our mess of life in the living room.

"Hey, Crispin,"

'Yeah?" I was smacking the board to the wall to get it to stick.

"I didn't walk into that club by accident."

I stopped and turned with my eyebrow raised. "What do you mean?"

"I mean, Fern and Jaggar told me about the club. They were the ones that recommended that I go there. Fern even gave me a ticket to get in. I wouldn't have been able to get past the entrance without it."

I sat, leaving the board halfway hung up, while she started tapping on the table nervously. I let the initial anger wash hit me and brushed through it before asking questions. "What do you mean?"

"I mean, they saw me when I went to smoke, and I was pissed at you, and I asked them if they knew of any good clubs."

"Jaggar and Fern? Like my vampire cousin and his vampire girlfriend?" I folded my hands together, trying to sound calm. "Why didn't you tell me?"

"I don't know. I was hungover, and then I got nervous." I could see her anxiety building, so I just nodded. My cousin was going to die.

Okay, maybe not die, but he would have some serious questions to answer. He would know Maisie wasn't supposed to be in a vampire club. My mind ran through every possibility of him not knowing, or maybe he assumed that's what Maisie meant when she asked for recommendations. Either way, he and Fern lied when they told me they didn't know where Maisie went.

Why the hell would they lie? Why would they send Maisie off to a vampire club and then lie to my face about not knowing where she was?

"Okay, well, I'll have to talk to him about it the next time we see him." I nodded at her, hoping to communicate that I was not going to fly off the handle.

"You're not going to punch him?"

"I mean, Darcy says an open palm slap is more dramatic. But it's not cool that they would tell you to go there, Mais."

"I know. I just know we've already caused a lot of trouble. I don't want to accuse him of something that might be a misunderstanding."

"I'm not going to call anyone, but you bet your ass the next time I see him, I'll talk to him."

"Just talk," she reminded me, and I held my pinky out. She laced her pinky in mine, and we shook on it.

Sixteen

Maisie

"Tell me why cutting down our Christmas tree is a good idea when there is a perfectly good lot like a mile from our house?" I complained as I pulled the scarf up and around my face.

November had passed without much incident. We even spent Thanksgiving with my parents, who hosted a large get-together. Crispin had been pleasant enough, though when my father talked to him, he sent me distressed eyes, and I had to go save him. We hadn't seen Jaggar or Fern since the Halloween party, but we probably wouldn't until closer to Christmas. It was the first week of December, and Crispin had insisted it was time to cut our own tree in the dense evergreen forest about forty minutes away from our house.

"Think of the pictures and caption for our first Christmas. It's like Jessica's wet dream. We can take a picture in front of it with some hot chocolate." He had a chainsaw hefted over his shoulder that he had borrowed from his dad. And I tried not to notice how good he looked in black jeans, a black sweater, and a green calf-length wool coat. I had ordered the coat for some of our fancier parties, and now he wore it to everything.

"I don't know what you and Jessica's deal is."

"It's mutual disrespect," he said, stopping and looking to see if he could spot the tree we would take home.

Crispin and I had become friends in the past few weeks, much better friends than we ever had been. Our teasing had returned to its flirtatious nature, and we had fun together.

Friends.

Friends that slept together.

Nothing had ever happened, but we now had an unspoken understanding, whether in my bed or Crispin's—It didn't really matter. We always woke up a tangled mess, and in the past week, we had become slower and slower to unravel.

Also, in the past week, my thoughts had been wandering. I found myself focusing on his mouth when he talked or flushing when he complimented me. I tried to tell myself that no good could come from feeling like this. We would never survive the next four years and change things if something went romantically sideways.

"I could just take off into these trees back to the truck and leave you to drag the tree yourself," I mused, looking back to the truck, but I couldn't see through the forest. I was cold, and I really didn't think this whole scraggly tree from the middle of nowhere thing was for me.

"I'd catch you," he said it absently as if he were only half listening, but his words sent a spike of heat through me, whether he had meant them to or not.

"I'm faster than you; I've seen you run."

He then turned and became fully invested in the argument. "No, you've seen me run on a treadmill. When I try to appear as if I do not possess the ability to run faster than the average human."

"I've been trained." I walked past him, giving him a teasing smile. "I'm smaller, lighter, faster."

"Smaller, yes. Lighter, yes. Faster, no."

"I would lose you in this forest," I continued.

"No," he chuckled, and now there was a deepness to his words that edged on something I tried not to revel in. "You would not."

"I would; it's fine to have a wrong opinion." I turned back to see what my challenge had evoked. Laughter bubbled out of me to watch as he set the chainsaw down on the ground, and his eyes narrowed.

"You cannot possibly think that you would outrun me or lose me. I am a vampire, Maisie. You may be trained to fight, and your training is impressive as hell, but you lose this every time."

"Prove it," I dared him, my heart in my throat, my stomach erupting with butterflies.

"You want me to chase you through the woods?"

Goodness, yes. My brain supplied as I stared at him.

"Unless you aren't up for it." I let the insinuation work its way under his skin.

"And what do I get if I catch you?" he asked, but I could already tell he would do it.

"If you catch me, you pick your prize." I didn't trust myself to give him any ideas out loud. I took off my bulky scarf and large jacket and hung them over a rock without snow on it. "Let's go, Booker." I put my hair back with a pink scrunchie from my wrist.

"I'll eat you alive, Princess." He walked over to where I was, moving the chainsaw by the rock. He shrugged off his jacket.

The chill nipped at my face, but his words still warmed me, and he smiled at their effect, which must have been clear on my face. Crispin and I were both competitive. I played soccer all through middle and high school. Soccer girls were ruthless, savage even. It was a good way to get out my frustrations. And I'd seen Crispin play basketball more than my fair share. He played hard and was pissed when the team lost. Darcy and Erik played, but they weren't like Crispin— weren't like me. We understood the need to win. The board games I played with the Bookers and the virtual Scrabble I played with Trudy didn't really incite a thrill.

"I'll give you a thirty-second head start," he said, sitting on the large rock.

"I don't need a head start." I put my hands on my hips.

"Yeah, you do." He smiled at me, a flush on his own cheeks and a certain sparkle in his eyes. We stared at each other momentarily, and I wondered if his pulse was racing like mine. "Run, Mais." He didn't have to say anything else.

I turned and ran as fast as I could into the greenery beyond. I needed more than thirty seconds. I knew that. I had been trained to fight, but they had never given me false hope of beating a vampire. But I could at least give him a good run of it.

I heard him coming after me as my lungs burned from sprinting and taking in the cold hair. I'd gotten a little soft eating junk food with Crispin, and I didn't work out as much as I did before.

I was cursing myself now. But I kept pushing myself forward, through the trees. My snow boots weren't meant for sprinting, and I nearly fell half a dozen times. The foliage flew by me as I dodged branches and fallen debris that would slow me down. I would sprint as far as possible and then look for a hiding place. I pushed my body until I was panting, breathing ragged.

I slowed a minute and turned to look to see Crispin not far behind me.

"Shit," I said under my breath as I looked for a good place to hide as it was apparent that I just ran my ass off so he could basically jog and catch up with me. I hustled toward a tree out of the main path with a large enough trunk to hide behind. Once I made it through the brush, I tried to control my breathing.

I heard him approach. "You gotta do better than that, Pope. Where's all that big talk? I thought you were trained for this?" He mocked me, and my stomach fluttered again at his nearness.

He was coming up behind the tree—My tree. I sprinted off downhill, but I had little chance of escape. I veered for another trunk with low branches I could climb. I reached and grabbed one to pull myself up.

But before I could, his hands were on my waist, pulling me down, turning me around, and pinning me back against the tree.

"Gotcha."

I looked up at him, and the adrenaline in me spiked again. His fangs were out, and his eyes had shifted from tanzanite to garnet. He was breathing heavily, too, which made me feel a little better about how easily I had been captured.

"What will your prize be?" I panted, unsure if I was scared of him like this or not. Was it just the thrill of the challenge that made it kind of attractive? Probably just that and maybe a little bit of how he looked at me.

One thing I knew for sure was that no hunter should find being chased by a vampire as thrilling as I just had.

His red eyes shifted from my eyes to my lips, catching on them momentarily before moving to my neck and collarbone. I turned my head so that he had better access to it. His gaze flicked back to mine, surprised, as he hesitated. I hadn't seen this version of him before; even when he was angry, this was something else. Not anger, but hunger.

"Go ahead." My voice came out as a whisper, and he went statuesque before me.

What the hell was I thinking? Was I about to let Crispin Booker bite me in the middle of the woods? I couldn't deny that I was curious about how it felt. The warnings painted it as a deep well that one couldn't come back from. When humans were bitten, they begged their assailants to drink them dry. Would I beg him? The morbid side of me wanted to know.

He reached up and ran the backs of his two fingers along the exposed skin of my throat. I shivered and unintentionally flinched away a bit. He stepped away immediately.

"I wouldn't hurt you," he said like I had accused him.

His eyes had shifted back to blue, his fangs retracted, and his posture was defensive instead of predatory. I felt a trickle of guilt slither through me. I hadn't meant to recoil; it had just been instinct.

"I know."

A hollowness filled me. I didn't know if it was because he stepped back or because I was worried I had created an emotional distance between us. Maybe part of it was the heady realization that I had been very close to letting him sink his teeth into me with very little concern. I had been too overwhelmed by the feelings that had been building and bubbling.

"Are you sure?" He gave me a smile, but the problem was that I could tell which ones were fake now. He'd just given me a smile reserved for rich people's parties.

He took a half-step forward, reached over my head, and tugged something in my hair. At first, I thought that it was a twig or something that had gotten caught in it while I was running. He gently removed my scrunchie. He slipped it onto his wrist and shook it a little before me.

"You said I could pick my prize." He didn't wait for me to say anything as he turned around. "Let's go find a Christmas tree."

Seventeen

Crispin

I was not doing good.

Since that day in the woods a week ago, my thoughts had been out of control. I was drinking more blood than normal just to make sure I wasn't hungry at any time around Maisie. However, despite that, my mind still wandered. I had even pretended to fall asleep on our couch three times playing video games, so I didn't have to wake up pressed against her.

I absolutely hated it because I liked sleeping next to her. But I did not like thinking about sinking my fangs into her soft skin every time her throat was exposed or when she bent over in the kitchen. I had never felt need like this before. I had liked girls, but Maisie was the first one I'd ever kissed or slept next to. First, I ever actually caught feelings for.

Because the truth was that I was in deep here with Maisie now, the affection of friendship had morphed into something else, and that day, when I had her pinned against that tree, when she tilted her head to let me bite her, the vampire in me had become acutely aware of her presence.

It had come to the point where I was referring to myself and my vampirism as separate people. Because I didn't want to take responsibility for the feral way I had been thinking about things.

I told her I needed a day with my brother, so she made plans with Trudy and Briar to see a movie and hang out at the mall. I pulled up to my parents' driveway on edge, like I had been for the last week. I slammed my truck door harder than I needed to and stomped to the front door. I felt a little lightheaded and off, like I may have been getting sick, but I needed to talk to someone before I exploded.

"Take it easy on the doors, man," Darcy said from the living room, where he watched me walk in and shut the door behind me.

"Please tell me you have everything set up," I pleaded, then sighed as I saw he had our old system all out.

"Briar, didn't mind me coming over?" I took a seat next to him and sank back into the familiar couch.

"No, Dude, honestly, I think she was getting a little sick of me. She's on edge with all the schoolwork she has to do for her electrical stuff. It's good she's hanging with the girls."

"I didn't know Briar got sick of you." I snorted, but I supposed it made sense. Briar had a short fuse and a limited amount of patience.

"Oh yeah, I mean, she irritates me sometimes too. We are different people, and we deal with things differently." He shrugged.

I was slightly surprised to hear him say it but also a little proud. Our parents taught us that relationships were hard work and that we had to choose our partners daily. There would always be bumps in the road, but your person was your person. Darcy would never speak negatively about Briar, but the brother trust zone was unbreakable.

"You guys good?" I asked, trying to be as casual as I could.

"Yeah, totally good. We've just been working some things out. She's getting better at not lashing out when I unintentionally hurt her feelings, and I'm getting better about not just going along with whatever she says to keep her happy. It's just a process, you know? But we are all good." He nodded, and I saw him relax a little.

"Yeah, well, I don't think there could be two people as different as you guys, but you're good for each other." I reached for a gaming headset.

"Yeah, I think so too."

I waited for him to say more or start the game, but he did not.

"So?" he questioned, and I realized he was waiting for me to say something.

"So?" I shrugged, knowing exactly what he was waiting for. To my point, he tilted his head and gave me an incredulous look.

"Did you just share that with me so I would share with you?" I shook my head in disbelief.

"Not exactly. I needed to tell someone, and I'm not sharing stuff about Briar with anyone who wouldn't get that I love her. But I still need to talk, you know? Also, when you text and say we need a game day, I know something is up."

"I'm that predictable?" I set the gaming headset down and leaned back into the couch.

"Maybe not to other people, but we've shared the same space for like eighteen years." He shrugged, and I exhaled.

"I want to bite Maisie so bad I can't even be in the same room with her without thinking about it," I said it all in one breath and then felt like a dick for admitting it out loud.

"Did something happen to make it bad, or just over time?" he asked me, and as usual, there was no hint of judgment.

"Something happened," I affirmed, but I wasn't about to go into the details.

He ran his hands through his hair thoughtfully. Briar was a human, so I hoped Darcy would understand. Vampires didn't crave vampire blood. The vampire disease changed something about it so that it no longer satisfied cravings. I wasn't sure Dad would understand; otherwise, he would have been my first call.

"Do you bite Briar?" I asked, hoping it wasn't an overstep.

"No. I mean, other than the two times." He waved his hand. Darcy had bitten her once on accident at school when she kissed him and once when he had been stabbed and needed fresh blood to survive. "But not like I wouldn't; I just haven't. I guess I'm a little afraid. You've always been better than me in controlling that part of you."

"I wouldn't say that," I thought of the blood pouring from Ajay's nose.

"Crispin, I bit Briar in the hallway of the school and nearly ripped her damn throat open."

"You were hungry," I defended.

"Doesn't matter. I don't think I'd hurt her. I just don't bite her. Not that she's against it, I don't think. But we also haven't had sex."

"You haven't?" I wasn't sure if I was surprised or not.

"Nah, neither of us is in a hurry. But before we did, I would probably bite her a few times so that I wasn't overwhelmed with the desire while it was happening. Are you guys...," He trailed off, looking at me, hoping I would pick up what he meant.

"Not yet." I shook my head.

"But not yet means it could happen." He picked up his gaming headset. "I wouldn't wait for it to happen at the same time. Maisie could hold her own, and I don't think you would hurt her, but you know...just to be safe."

This conversation had gone wildly different than I had anticipated. Then again, I hadn't come here expecting to open up to my brother about everything all at once. Part of me had just wanted to play mindless video games until it went away. Another part of me had known Darcy would make me talk. That's why I needed him.

Now I was thinking about how to prep my hunter girlfriend in case we ever decided to do more than just sleep next to each other. Did she even want that? What was in her eyes that day in the woods suggested she did, but maybe that was just a one-time thing. Or maybe I had completely missed the mark, and there had been no desire there to begin with, only fear.

I was going to have to ask her outright.

Eighteen

Maisie

"What does it feel like to be bitten?" I asked rather suddenly as soon as Trudy disappeared out the theater doors to go to the bathroom.

The movie was still playing, and I had forcefully whispered to Briar, worried this was the only time we would have alone.

She raised her head to me, lifted her eyebrow, and put some popcorn into her mouth. She didn't answer my question, and the longer she stared, the warmer my cheeks became. Damn, she had a way of making people uncomfortable. She finally turned her head back to the screen.

"Why are you asking?" Her response was also a whisper, even though the theater was nearly empty except for an older couple all the way at the back.

"Just curious."

"I'm sure." She chuckled, and I folded my arms, facing forward once more.

"Fuck off." I should have known that she wouldn't help me. She just seemed to revel in my misery.

"I don't know how to describe it to you," she said finally. "It's better than any feeling I could think to compare it to, and in the moment, you'd let them kill you. You'd have to trust him, because you may beg him to keep going when he needs to stop."

I shivered at the finality of her answer and didn't press any further. Her words were exactly what I was worried about.

I felt things had been off with Crispin and me since that day in the forest. I worried I had ruined what we had because it had started to feel like a place I was safe in. I didn't have many people with whom I could truly relax. My whole childhood, I had felt on edge around my parents. Only when I met Trudy did I feel like I'd met someone who understood me, someone I didn't have to have my guard up all the time. Crispin had seen my anxiety; he'd seen me a complete mess, and he'd cleaned throw-up out of my hair, for goodness sake. He'd started to feel a little like I imagined home should feel like.

Then, this past week, he'd slept on the couch several times. When I made eye contact with him, his gaze was strained, and his posture was stiff. Why was everything with him so damn hard? Whenever we took a couple of steps forward, something seemed to knock us on our asses.

Anytime I had worked up the courage to talk to him about it, I would find him, and my anxiety would make it so my words stuck in my throat. Then, today, when I asked him what he wanted to do, he told me he needed to hang out with Darcy. He was an idiot if he thought I couldn't tell he was ignoring me.

When the movie was over, the girls and I went to a local burger place, where they discussed their schoolwork and jobs. Trudy talked a bit about Erik's stuff he had going on and excitedly babbled about how she thought he might propose soon. She cutely played with her braids while she talked about him. Even though she and Erik had been together since freshman year, they were still just as in love as they always had been. No one in the school doubted that they would end up together.

"What about you and Darcy?" Trudy asked our salty friend, who, after rolling her eyes, gave us minimal updates on her and Darcy's relationship. She also gave us updates on Triana, her best friend who had moved away for college. Trudy and I tried to check in on Briar more frequently now because we knew Triana's moving was hard on her, but she would never say that to us.

We chatted, ate, said our goodbyes, and headed home. On the way home, I listened to a little bit of Crispin's vampire podcast about the emotions of young vampires. I had learned that teenage vampires had the strongest emotions, were the most sensitive, and needed the most blood, but they were also the strongest. Guilt started creeping up in me about being hard on Crispin for being angry. Part of it had to do with the vampirism disease.

He had been so patient with me through my anxiety attacks and moments of immobility. I treated his emotional reactions like an annoying inconvenience, expecting him to get a grip. That isn't how he treated me when my worry crept up my throat and drowned out all logical thought. He'd never made me feel like that, even if he thought it. Were our emotions all that different? To some extent, they controlled us and made our lives more difficult.

I had always viewed my anxiety as a problem; Crispin had just made me feel like it was part of me. Not good or bad, but just there. Even if he felt like it was draining him, he had never let me see him feel that way. He was gentle with me. I realized that was why pulling into our parking spot in front of our condo was like coming home. Being with him was like sloughing off all my exterior pretending and being allowed to be myself. Stupid tears formed in my eyes as I shut off the podcast and sat for a minute in my car, cracking the window to smoke.

I looked over and saw Crispin's car. I was surprised that he was already home from his day with Darcy. I wanted to go into our house and kiss his stupid face—for a lot of reasons.

Some part of me had always liked Crispin. He had been right that day in Seattle. We had flirted with each other for the entire time we had known each other in school. Even though Trudy had been shocked and angry when I first announced we were getting married, she had admitted she had wanted to yell *JUST KISS ALREADY* at us several times when our bickering became unbearable. But flirting with him in high school had been safe. I knew they were vampires almost immediately because of the tabs we kept on their kind. I knew that nothing could have ever happened between us.

It had become decidedly less safe, and the fluttering in my stomach when he was near had become a problem. When I thought of his tenderness to me and the way we had grown closer, the issue became a Godzilla-scale threat.

My guarded heart was like the city of Tokyo, and Crispin was like an oversized lizard that reigned atomic breath.

When I made my way into the house, feeling jumbled and still not sorted out, I found Crispin curled up on the couch. A bowl of instant ramen and a mug of tea were in front of him, and Pride and Prejudice from ninety-five was playing on the TV. Only his face was visible through a hole in a fluffy white blanket that stretched around his whole frame.

"Don't judge me," he muttered before he could even see me, and I let out a chuckle.

"You okay?" I asked as he wiggled around until he could see my face.

"I didn't feel great this morning, and it got worse when I was with Darcy, so I cut out early. I'm cold, and I think I have a fever."

"Man flu," I tsked. "A terrible epidemic."

He scoffed, wiggling back to watch the TV. When I went over and felt his forehead, he was warm, but I didn't know if it was because he was wrapped like a burrito or because he was sick.

"Can I watch with you?" I asked, stepping back.

Instead of answering, he pulled his feet back to make room for me on the couch.

He *was* sick and was less of a baby than some men I had encountered, but still...a bit dramatic.

After a few hours of period dramas and a romantic comedy, he took a shower and crawled into bed. As I was no chef, I made him some canned soup. I heated him another cup of tea and got some nighttime cold and flu medicine I found in the medicine cabinet. The Order and The Guild had it well stocked with all the goods.

I set everything on his nightstand and noticed the pink scrunchie he had stolen from me. It sparked heat to color my cheeks as I remembered Crispin's fingers slowly dragging down my throat. I shook the memory off and took a shower myself.

After my *everything* shower, I got into my pajamas and tied my hair up in a silk scarf. I climbed into my own bed and turned the lights off, trying to be quiet, assuming Crispin had fallen asleep.

I was wrong, and his form appeared in the doorway of my room. "What are you doing?"

He startled me a bit, so I sat up abruptly.

"Scrolling on my phone." My tone was defensive, as I didn't understand what he meant.

"Why aren't you sleeping with me?"

Geez, thank goodness the room was dark.

"Because you're sick?" I questioned.

"You're worried you'll get sick?"

"No, I just thought you might sleep better without me in there?"

"That's stupid. Come on," he demanded in a half-delirious voice.

After a minute, I followed him and slid into his bed. His breathing became deeper as he lay flat on his back, and I lay next to him, scrolling on my phone again.

"Hey, Mais?" he asked after a few minutes.

"Yeah?" I turned my head to look at him. His eyes were closed, and his voice had that groggy quality.

"There's not really a not awkward way for me to ask this, but like...are we going to kiss or sleep together? Not now, like eventually in the future?"

Godzilla strike me down.

"We are sleeping together," I said after too long, and it came out sort of strangled.

He sighed as if exasperated. "Listen, we absolutely don't have to. But if we do, it won't be normal, like with a normal person. Like when you were with Ajay. We will have to be more careful and take more precautions. But I just need to know what you want and what you don't."

"Are you high?" I whispered this to him, though it was only him and me. I was flushed again, and not just my face. I felt like I had a fever, too.

"A little, that cold medicine makes me feel like I'm swimming."

"Maybe we should talk about this later," I suggested, willing him to agree so I could stop feeling like I was having the most awkward conversation of my life.

"Let's just get it over with right now."

"I don't know what you want me to say." I felt lightheaded. What if I said something wrong? What if I didn't know exactly what I wanted right now? What if I hurt his feelings or insinuated something that made him feel like I was scared of him—like I had last week?

"Listen, let's start easy. I want to kiss you. Do you want to kiss me?" His voice was so soft and hopeful it made my chest squeeze.

I want to die right now is what I want to do.

"Why do we have to talk about this?" I groaned, putting a pillow on top of my face. My default was to always shove things down and pretend things weren't happening. This was the opposite of that.

"Because I want you to feel safe. I don't want to do anything you don't want to do. But I'm walking around this house on the edge of pushing you up against the counter and either kissing you or biting you. So let's just talk about what we want to happen so stuff doesn't happen... we don't want." His words were also choppy and awkward, as if he were trying to work through how to say them himself. Why was nineteen such a weird age to be? We weren't kids anymore but this conversation sure as hell felt like the awkward admission of a crush.

Oh, what the hell.

"Yeah, I want to kiss you." I lifted the pillow so it wouldn't be muffled. "Also, I think about you biting me. A lot. And not in...." I struggled. "Not in a scary way. Like when we went to get our tree, I wanted you to bite me. I might have been a little scared, but mostly...not scared."

He let out a slow breath, and the silence was heavy after that.

"Okay, well."

"Well," I parroted.

I was beyond embarrassed. I had just admitted to a vampire that I wanted him to bite me. What would my father say?

After Crispin said nothing, I heard his breathing deepen.

"Are you seriously sleeping?" I asked, smacking the pillow I was holding over his head. He let out a low chuckle. He shifted quickly and moved closer to me. I turned in anticipation as he pulled me to him.

"I've never had a girl say they wanted me to kiss them before."

Tokyo -0 Godzilla-1

Nineteen

Crispin

When I got out of the shower after our gym circuit, Maisie was on the porch smoking a cigarette. She had run hard at the gym for longer than I had. She lifted the weights like it was her life's mission and didn't notice anyone or anything else.

Then, as soon as we got home, she took her intensity out on the four dishes in the sink. I don't think any dishes had ever been cleaner. As I toweled off my hair, I could smell the distinct scent of an all-purpose cleaner and realized she had gone to town. I made my way out the front door in bare feet and stared at her as she strategically avoided my eyes.

"Talk to me, Pope." I reached out and tugged lightly on one of her curls.

We had plans to do all our grocery shopping and pick up the stuff for dinner with her family the next day. At least Maisie had already cleaned the apartment.

"It's an anxious day." She exhaled as if it pained her to admit it. I knew from being around her for a few months that she did, in fact, feel like admitting she was anxious felt like a failure.

"Ah, are you up to grocery shopping? Or do you want me to go?"

She lit another cigarette off her first one, which I found impressive.

"I should go with you," she said finally.

"You should do whatever is going to make you feel the best. I can go grocery shopping. If you want to stay here, shower, watch TV, or...clean all our already clean dishes." I smiled, and she shot me a sideways look.

"You don't mind? I can go...." She shrugged.

"You make a list of whatever you need, and I think I can handle it—unless you want me to stay home."

"No." She answered too fast and then cringed at how the words came out, but I just laughed.

She made me a list that filled a page and a half and slid it to me across the counter. I assured her I would be fine, and she eyed the underside of the couch as I threw on a hoodie and left the house.

Maisie's parents were coming over the next night for Christmas dinner.

We had a Christmas Eve Ball to go to. I thought it had just been a name for the party, but no. It was a whole white tie event and I had to get fitted for a suit with coattails. We would be out of town for Christmas as well, which I could tell my parents were a little bummed about. We would see Maisie's parents at the ball, but my parents weren't rich or influential enough to be invited.

I'd promised them brunch the week after, and they smiled and told me that would be fine. Darcy hadn't been happy about it either. It turns out the Bookers weren't *change* people, but they did support me, and so their unhappiness was limited to their facial expressions.

At the grocery store, I checked off all the items Maisie asked for while adding some of my favorites. I had learned that Maisie did not like generic brand versions of any foods. She claimed you could always tell the difference. I had grown up with a mom who taught me how to coupon and sale shop. Maisie shopped by convenience, no matter the cost. So, all the items on her list were the nicest version of that thing on the shelf. But I snagged generic cheese balls for a TV snack. I checked an app on my phone for coupons for the items I purchased.

I stopped at the floral section, picked out some white alstroemeria for our table, and almost bumbled into someone when I turned around.

"Sorry." The apology died in my throat when I saw who I was standing in front of.

Morgan Pope. My brother's girlfriend's ex. Maisie's cousin, who had helped kidnap Briar earlier in the year. He and his family had tried to get me and Darcy to violate vampire/hunter rules so they could take us out. His older brother and father had been put in hunter prison for their crimes, but Morgan had gotten a second chance.

Unfortunately.

"Oh, Crispin." He blanched a bit, and my mind flashed back to that moment where I had nearly pressed my blood into his open wound. I had burned with white rage and lost myself. I would have done it; his chances of turning after blood-to-blood contact were high. But Maisie's voice broke through, as I heard her begging me to spare him.

So now I had to see him at the grocery store—and I was having a good day before.

"Morgan." I looked him up and down but kept my posture soft. I wasn't looking to start a fight with him, for Maisie's sake.

"How is...married life?" He cringed a bit at his own question, and I didn't give him the satisfaction of saving him with an answer. I just pursed my lips and raised an eyebrow.

"Yeah." He rubbed the back of his neck. "Listen, Crispin."

I still didn't say anything.

"I'm sorry about everything that happened."

"A lot happened." I set the flowers in my cart, not making us suffer through more eye contact.

"Yeah," he said again, letting the word sit between us.

"Okay, well, good talk." I went to walk away, not wanting to bother with this asshat of a human anymore.

"Crispin," his tone was strained, and I could tell he was trying, so I turned back to look at him.

"I...." He stared at me as if I could understand something he hadn't said out loud. "I love my cousin and want her to be happy."

It wasn't what I thought he would say, and it took me off guard a bit. I didn't exactly know how to respond to the concern in his voice. Was he worried about her being in a fake marriage? Did he know she was? Or was he worried about her being around me? Without asking, I guess I'd never know.

"I hear you, man." I nodded as reassuringly as I could. "I want her to be happy too."

I was surprised to find that that was the truth. I wanted Maisie Pope-Booker to be happy and would do what I could to make that happen.

Morgan only nodded, and I went to check out, leaving him behind without any closing goodbye.

I wondered when I had stopped thinking of Maisie as the situation I would have to endure for five years and more like a person I wanted to defend. I couldn't pinpoint an exact moment, but Maisie had become more than a means to an end over time. She had become my friend and someone who I enjoyed being around. I wanted to be a good fake husband, take care of her, and protect her—without punching people in the face. I wanted to be her person. I wanted it in a way I hadn't wanted something before. After seeing how her parents treated her and how close she kept everything. I wanted to be the person she could relax around.

These thoughts drove me as I stopped at a garden center on my way home. It was one of my mom's favorite places around Christmas time. They had a million trees decorated to the nines, and they usually had color-coordinated trees. Since we hadn't decorated our tree yet, I thought I might pick Maisie up a few pink ornaments for our first Christmas together.

Sure enough, the place had an entirely pink tree in the back, and I smiled, thinking of how much Maisie would like it. I took a picture and texted it to her. Not thirty seconds later, she sent me what looked like twenty-five star-eyed emojis.

"Do you need help finding anything?" A short older woman with salt and pepper hair came up from behind me.

"Well." I looked at her name tag on her blue apron. "Debbie, I think I need every ornament on this tree, that flamingo tree topper, and some of the pink lights if you have them."

The Guild and The Order were about to buy Maisie an entire pink Christmas tree set up.

"What is this?" Maisie peered into the brown tissued bags. I'd waited to bring them in until the groceries were sorted and the flowers were in a vase to not overwhelm her with one hundred things at once.

"For our tree." I shrugged, suddenly feeling embarrassed for reasons I didn't understand.

She unwrapped a bubblegum-colored glass ornament first. "Oh my gosh, it's gorgeous."

"You have about fifty to unwrap, so get to it," I said, going to the cabinet to grab some microwave popcorn.

She ogled every single one at an excruciating pace. Maisie was a present girl, and while the opening rate was a little maddening, it was worth seeing her face light up with each new ornament. When she got to the lights, she rushed to the tree immediately, and we strung them on. Then, she placed every ornament by herself, and found them the perfect spot. There were forty-two ornaments, a box full of pink tree bows, and a pink gingham tree skirt.

When she was done, it looked so much like her that I stared at it and laughed. She smacked me on the arm, but not before giving me a huge smile.

For lunch, we ate sandwiches on the couch while watching some terrible reality TV show in which the couples were forced to get married without meeting each other first.

"I love my tree," she said without looking at me.

"You want to talk about what you're freaking out over?" I asked in response.

She took a bite of her sandwich and talked around her food. "Nope."

I reached for her free hand nearest to me and laced my fingers into hers. "I think we would have made good contestants on this show."

"We are just dramatic enough for views," she agreed, her warm hand squeezing mine twice.

Twenty

Maisie

I woke up thirty minutes early every day to stare at my tree with a cup of coffee on the couch. It was one thing that made the condo feel like it was ours. It wasn't a whitewashed generic space anymore; it was personal. I was really excited for my parents to come and see it, though I wouldn't admit it out loud. Somehow, when you acknowledged expectations, they were constantly smashed.

Crispin and I sat on the sofa that evening on a Zoom with Jessica as she went over exactly what we would be doing after we got off the plane for our holiday tour.

"Christmas Eve is the Novic's ball, held in the ballroom of the hotel you are staying at, for convenience."

"That was thoughtful." Crispin mused, and Jessia shot him a look through the screen. She thought he was being an asshole, which was fair.

"The Haymaks will have you over Christmas Eve morning for brunch at their estate. They are hunters, old ones, important ones." She directed all these words at Crispin, and I bit my lip to cover a smile.

"Don't fuck this up, Crispin, got it." He saluted her, and she let out a deep sigh.

"My expectations are not high," she scolded, looking at something on her phone and mumbling to herself as if she were checking things off a list.

"You come home the day after Christmas following having breakfast with Crispin's grandfather on Christmas day." I felt Crispin stiffen beside me, but he didn't say anything.

"Your social media presence has been lacking; we need more posts and more looks into your everyday lives. More physical affection needs to be present," she said all this like it was a clinical demand, but my face warmed.

"We can do that," Crispin said, bumping my shoulder. Jessica looked up from her phone to give him another withering glare.

"I think that's all. Of course, you both have my number in case you need me."

"Do you get paid well to babysit us, Jess?" Crispin leaned forward, toward the camera, and called our handler by a name she hated.

"Not nearly enough, Mr. Booker." She signed off without another word, leaving Crispin with a shit-eating grin.

"I think she's warming up to me."

"How do I look?" I asked, coming out of the bathroom as I jittered with nerves. I told my parents it was a casual dinner, so I was wearing matching pink sweats that I had considered changing at least one hundred times.

Crispin peered over at me, where he was arranging a cheese board exactly the way I had asked him to. He wore jeans and a blue sweater, with a gold necklace and gold hoop earrings. He had put on one white and one black sock, which I found terribly charming for some reason.

"Great! You look comfortable."

"My mom will probably tell me I look sloppy." I played with the sleeve of my top.

"Oh well." He shrugged, never thinking about what people would think about him. Or maybe he just didn't care what my parents thought of him.

I returned to the bathroom and added some small dangling pearl earrings and a necklace to make myself look less...comfortable. I brushed mascara over my eyelashes and spritzed myself with perfume before looking at my reflection and deciding it was as good as it would get.

I flew around the kitchen from one project to another, not getting anything done because I was nervous. Still, Crispin followed behind me and finished everything I started without saying anything until my parents rang our doorbell.

"Listen, Mais." Crispin grabbed me by the shoulders before I could run to answer the door. "Just chill out a little bit; it's going to be great. The food looks fantastic. You look lovely, and I look fabulous," he said, and I rolled my eyes. "Seriously, though, just remember, no matter how they make you feel, I love you, okay?"

He squeezed my shoulders and let go, turning toward the door, but I was still frozen in place. Right where he had left me.

How dare he say he loved me and let my parents into our house without addressing it.

Did he love me?

"What the hell, Crispin?" I got out just as he reached the door.

"I didn't mean it like that. I just meant it... platonically. Maybe in that other way, too, but I'm not sure yet." He hesitated, looking up at the ceiling like it held the answers. "But one hundred percent in the platonic friend way, I definitely love you." He babbled and opened the door before I could tell him what an idiot he was.

What we had didn't feel like platonic friendship, but I wasn't sure what it felt like.

"Mr. and Mrs. Pope, you look great tonight," he said, opening the door and banishing all hope of me working through anything right then.

My parents stepped in and didn't even try to pretend like they weren't inspecting the apartment. My mom glanced over at the tree, her eyes wide, and frowned. She was not a big fan of my signature color.

"Maisie and I decorated that. I think we did a fantastic job," Crispin said, breezing past my mother. "Can I get you guys something to drink? We have sparkling water, regular water, or some cool mocktails Maisie created."

"I'll take one," my dad said, stopping next to me, looking like he might hug me, but he just nodded instead. "This is a nice place."

"Yeah, we like it." I nodded.

"We?" he inquired, and I scrunched my face in confusion. "Yeah, Crispin and I?"

"I brought you kiddos something cute," my mom said, rummaging in her bag after setting her handful of bagged presents on the counter. She finally produced a small brown box with a clear window in the front. Crispin looked at it with a quizzical brow as if he couldn't figure out what it was.

"It's real mistletoe. They were selling them at this gorgeous tree farm in wine country."

"Oh, I don't think I've ever seen the real thing before." Crispin nodded as my mom took the sprig out of the box. "Well, come here." She waved me over to stand next to Crispin.

"The real way to use mistletoe is to pull off a berry every time someone kisses under it. Once all the berries are gone, it's all used up," my mom explained as if it were the most romantic thing she had ever heard.

"Helena, please don't." My dad cringed.

"Oh, hush, William. It's just a bit of fun." Mom said as she reached the mistletoe as high as she could manage over our heads from behind us. "You know what to do."

Crispin leaned closer to me as I was about to melt under the scrutiny of my parents and pressed a kiss to my cheek. Before I could die of embarrassment, he snatched the mistletoe from my mom and held it over her head. Quick as he could, he bent down to kiss her cheek, too. My mom turned a bright shade of pink and giggled, covering her mouth. I don't think I had ever heard my mom giggle before.

"You have to be careful with that stuff, Helena. It's dangerous." Crispin snatched two berries off it and handed them to her before throwing the mistletoe haphazardly onto one of the counters behind him. "Let's get you a drink."

"You are just as charming as your mother was," my mom said suddenly, and I froze, reaching for the presents to put them under our tree.

"Your grandfather used to bring her to parties and things when she was young, and you couldn't help but love her." Her tone was gentle in a way that made my chest sort of ache. I wanted her to use that tone more with me but I had so rarely heard it.

I looked over to Crispin, who stared at her for a moment.

"Thank you," he finally said with a small smile, but at least it was genuine.

I put presents under the tree, and my mom and dad sat in the living room. I heard my dad say something to my mom under his breath, and I could tell he was chastising her.

"I'm just feeling sentimental, that's all," she defended herself, and I spent longer than I needed to rearrange ornaments.

Dinner went off surprisingly well, with Crispin even managing to talk with my dad about baseball. The creamy pesto chicken and roasted tomatoes I made turned out great despite my worry that they wouldn't. I think I read the recipe one hundred times before I attempted it.

We sat in the living room to open presents. We got my parents a framed picture of them from the wedding. They got me a spa package from my mom's favorite place, a new pair of pink sneakers, and some fancy kitchen gadgets I wasn't sure about using. I thanked them and then waited while Crispin opened his gift from them. It was a sweater, cashmere by the look of it, in a light blue.

"Oh, this might be the nicest sweater I've ever owned," he said, holding it up to himself.

I thought it wasn't a particularly thoughtful gift, and then realized my gifts weren't exceptionally thoughtful either. They were certainly nice. But the spa was my mother's favorite. The shoes were cute, but a size and a half too large, and the kitchen appliance was also odd. Perhaps I was overthinking it, but as I started assessing all the gifts my parents had gotten me throughout my life, I recognized the pattern.

To be fair, I had no idea what to get my parents, and Crispin remembered that we had a great picture from the photographer and suggested we get it framed for them. It was another way the thoughtfulness of his gesture showed up next to my experiences.

Crispin excused himself to use the restroom as I picked up tissue paper.

"Maisie," my dad said in a low voice, and I stopped what I was doing to look over at him. "Maisie, are you sleeping with that boy?"

"William, really?" my mother shout-whispered at him.

"Dad," I warned. He had never asked me anything like this before. He and my mom hadn't even had any sort of bird and bees talk with me. They had left that to the public education system.

"I want to know, when I came in here, you said *we* like you guys were together. Then, when he kissed you, you blushed." His voice was demanding, and my mother stared at him with an open mouth.

I didn't answer him. I just stood there amongst the graveyard of wrapping paper, willing the right answer to come to me. *Not right now, Dad, but I might soon.* No, probably not the right answer.

"I don't think he's a bad kid, Maisie. But he's a vampire, and you know how they are."

"How are they?" Crispin asked, walking calmly into the living room.

The air was so thick with tension that I thought I might suffocate as my dad trained his ire on Crispin.

"Unpredictable," my father finally ground out.

"Well, not all vampires, but you are definitely spot on with me, William." I watched as Crispin took a deep, calming breath, and I was so proud of him. I wanted to give him a thumbs-up.

My dad needed a thumbs down.

Crispin asked my mom if she wanted a tour of the back, awkwardly breaking the tension. I gave him an appreciative look, and he nodded slightly, doing a mock realtor voice as he explained the small apartment to my mother.

"So?" my dad asked me once they were out of earshot.

I sighed. Why couldn't he drop it?

"You're not that stupid, are you? I didn't raise you to be stupid, Maisie."

Tears threatened as his words cracked open all the ways he knew how to make me feel insecure. The nerves that had wound their way up yesterday and today felt so tight in my chest that I couldn't breathe.

"Dad, just stop."

"Do you seriously want to play with your life like that?" he hissed.

The nerves snapped, and I stood up straight, facing him.

"You are the one who asked me to do this," I said firmly.

"Lower your voice." He looked startled. *Good*.

"No. You and Mom asked me to do this. You told me it would be good for the family, good for you. If you hadn't told me to, I wouldn't have agreed to it. Now, I am the one sacrificing five years of my life, Dad. Crispin is sacrificing five years of his life, while you benefit from this while doing nothing."

"Maisie Marie Pope," he demanded as if pulling out my full name was going to stop me now.

"What Crispin and I do is our business because you didn't seem to care about my welfare when you asked me to be married to a vampire for five years. You don't get to care all of a sudden."

"I'll take that as a yes to my question then." His voice had gone quiet, but it still held a steel edge.

"Take it however you want." I didn't falter or look away. Though, I could feel a sadness threatening to take me over as my dad and I stared at each other in silence. My breathing labored as

I tried to swallow the build-up of emotion in my throat. I didn't want to cry after standing up to him for the first time in my life.

"Oh my gosh, William, you have to see these," Moms voice came from the back as she held Crispin's laptop open.

"She asked about wedding photos." Crispin shrugged.

"Oh, darling, I do wish you would have worn white. It would have looked better on your skin, but you do look beautiful."

"Thanks, Mom." I turned as my mom set the laptop on the counter. She commented on all the photos until she was satisfied but I stared at mine and Crispin's faces. Smiles were plastered on, but if you knew how to look, you could tell we weren't happy. Now I wish we could do them over. But they were just fake photos, so what did it really matter?

There was a certain level of awkwardness the rest of the night between my dad and I, and his goodbye was clipped as he and my mother walked out the door. Once they were gone, I slipped back over to the laptop and looked through the pictures again as Crispin did the dishes. I was still sitting there when he got done.

"I think we need to frame one of those for the house or something," he said, looking over my shoulder.

"No," I said it so finally and decidedly that he pulled back a little.

"Alright. What, you don't like the tuxedo?"

I stood up and pulled out my phone going to my music app as I searched for the song we danced to at our wedding.

"Will you dance with me?" I asked, playing Too Marvelous for Words by Ella Fitzgerald. Resolution filled me as I determined what might be able to redeem those awful pictures and the knot of disappointment in my stomach.

"What?" He laughed, but it was sort of breathy and unsure. "Why?"

"I just...." I faltered as my dad's words swirled in my head, and my feelings for Crispin mashed together in an uncomfortable symphony within me. "Our first dance kind of sucked."

He wasn't laughing anymore as he walked forward and pulled me into him.

The way we danced in the middle of our apartment wasn't showy or performative. It wasn't a display to anyone else except ourselves, and as his warm hand held mine while the other grazed the small of my back, I closed my eyes and rested against him. The music filled the space as I focused on the sound of Crispin's heartbeat and nothing else.

I couldn't undo those wedding pictures, but I could make better memories now.

The song ended, and I pulled back to look up at him. "Just wanted a redo, you know?"

He tucked a strand of hair behind my ear with a soft smile.

Twenty-One

Crispin

I just wanted a redo, you know?

I knew exactly what she meant, and as she looked up at me, I thought of all the things I wanted to redo, too. But one thing was the most pressing to me at that moment.

Maybe it was how she was looking at me through her lashes or how she smiled when I gave her mom a tour instead of tearing into her dad. Maybe it was the way that *she* tore into her dad. When I learned she only agreed to this crazy thing because her parents had asked her to—I hoped she didn't think I felt that was a dumb reason; I'd do pretty much anything for my parents, too. Though I had to admit it was pretty crappy that they had asked her in the first place. I knew my parents would never ask it of me if I hadn't wanted to.

"I have something I want a redo on." I pulled away and made my way into the kitchen. I shuffled through drawers looking for something.

Drawer after drawer, I rummaged through as Maisie came over and eyed my savage attempt to locate what I needed. I finally pulled out tape and swung around, locating the mistletoe on the counter where I had thrown it earlier. She watched, amused, as I walked to a wall in the living room and slapped the greenery up with haphazard abandon.

"Well, that looks horrible." Maisie's mouth quirked up at the awkward placement. It was crooked, and I didn't think the tape would win the battle in the end.

Her smile fell when I came and grabbed her shoulders, leading her over to it and pushing her against the wall directly underneath.

"Oh." She blanched when it dawned on her what my redo was.

I slid one of my hands behind her neck and nearly sighed at the way my fingers tangled in her hair. The silky feel of her curls wrapped around my fingers felt better than it should have. I brought my other hand to the side of her face, tipping her chin up to look at me.

Her cheeks were tinged pink, her mouth open slightly.

Fuck. She was pretty, and I was in way over my head.

"I'm most sorry for the way I kissed you after our wedding dance. I was being an asshole. But since there are berries left on this holiday plant. Guess I get at least one do over and maybe more if you don't mind it." Heat colored my own cheeks and spread all through me, making me feel dizzy.

"Agreed, you were definitely an asshole." She nodded, the words whispered as her eyes were trained on my lips.

"Will you bite me again?" I asked, remembering how vicious her retaliation had been that day.

"I think the better question is, are you going to bite me." Her return was a smile small and unsure. However, the desire I thought I had imagined before was plain as day in her eyes now. The vampire in me reveled in the realization.

"Do you want me to bite you?" I grinned as her heart rate spiked and her eyes flicked to my teeth. "No fangs tonight, Pope. I just want this to be...."

I leaned forward, not bothering to finish the thought because, honestly, I wasn't sure what I had been about to say.

This wasn't a slow kiss like in some movies. Where the man leans in a little, and the girl leans in, too. I pulled her slightly forward, but my mouth came down on hers without warning. I gently pressed into her, letting her decide whether she liked it or not.

I burned from the inside out as she tilted her head and pressed her lips to my bottom one. Before I lost my mind, I pulled back a little and reached up to pull one berry off the plant. My hand came down to wrap around her waist.

There wasn't any more hesitation in her gaze; there was sureness, which scared the shit out of me.

"Two more." She reached up on her toes this time, her hand running up my neck, to the back of my head, her fingers tangling in my hair. As she pulled me down to her, my lips met her smirk.

This kiss wasn't as gentle. It held the same ferocity as the one from our first dance but none of the bitterness. Both hands found their way down, lower and lower, until I was brushing the bare skin of her back where her sweater rose up. I made a contented sound, kissing and nipping her bottom lip. Then, her fist closed around my sweater to pull me closer.

"Okay, I think that should have counted as more than one, but for the sake of the tradition, we are going to say one," I finally said, pulling away.

She reached up, tipping her head back to look as she tried to pull a berry off. She was too short to reach the rest of them now, but all my mind registered was her extended neck and the way she smelled like our laundry soap. The way that my lips felt slightly swollen and how she had consumed me.

"Need a step ladder?" I inquired, bringing my fingers up to brush her neck. She relaxed into my touch, and my hand cupped her cheek. She closed her eyes and nuzzled into me.

It wasn't lost on me that she had gone from looking like my touch might make her violently ill to this. Her eyes closed, her pink mouth kissing the soft part of my palm.

"It took us too long to do that." I decided, playing gently with her curls.

"Us?" she asked incredulously. "You. It took you too long." She poked my chest lightly.

"Why has the kissing responsibility fallen on my shoulders?"

"Because," she said, ending the argument.

I stepped back after a minute, giving her a little bit of space, but I reached down and wound my fingers into hers.

"I'm proud of you for sticking up to your dad."

Her lips pursed into a line. "You heard that?"

"I can hear a lot better than you." I shrugged. "I can also hear you sing in the shower, but like when you are trying to be quiet and not sing above the noise of the water."

She scoffed, and I grinned, glad to lighten the mood after the dad comment.

"Wanna go watch *Say Yes to the Dress* and eat ice cream?" she suggested.

"Only if I am allowed to judge how much these women are willing to spend on a single dress they will only wear once."

"Hey, my dress was four thousand five hundred." She defended and smacked my arm.

"For what reason? It looked like a very fancy nightgown." I was horrified but then came to my senses, realizing I may be insulting the way my wife looked at our wedding. "I mean beautiful, a beautiful, very silky nightgown with a lot of buttons."

"I think you should stop talking," she suggested.

I took her advice and instead pulled her in for another kiss.

Twenty-Two

Maisie

We sat on the plane, which was getting ready to land in the city outside of where we would be staying for the Christmas ball.

Traveling on Christmas Eve's Eve was not ideal, but Crispin had surprised me with a gift to open in the morning, saying his parents always let him and Darcy open one gift before Christmas.

It was a pink crewneck sweatshirt that said *In My Vampire Era* with tiny red embroidered bats. My parents would have absolutely hated it. I opened it immediately and put it on as Crispin beamed, a slight flush on his cheeks as I tossed my other sweatshirt to swap them out.

I turned to him now with his headphones on as he watched *The Good, The Bad, and The Ugly* on his phone. He turned to me when he realized I was staring at him. He popped one headphone out and raised an eyebrow at me.

"A Western?" I inquired, "Clint Eastwood?"

"I'm a man of many interests." He put his earbud back in. "And don't you dare speak a word against Clint. He's a national treasure."

I snorted and turned to watch the descent into the airport. Crispin gripped the armrest when the flight got a bit bumpy. He always did this, but now, I reached over, laced my hand in his, and squeezed twice.

My mind went back to our shared kisses, my face aflame as my body remembered precisely where he had touched me and, more importantly, where he hadn't. My husband hadn't done much more than kiss me since then. His fingers would graze my arms or my neck, but the past couple of days, he always pulled away before anything more happened.

I was starting to get frustrated. I didn't want to make him uncomfortable, but I just didn't know if he was holding back on my account or his. I would get to the bottom of it before our first breakfast tomorrow.

The Henry was a beautiful hotel, and our suite was another gorgeous two-bedroom unit with a large bathroom featuring a clawfoot tub.

We set our luggage down, and Crispin immediately went to the snack bar and fridge, which was always his first move. Watching him drink a Blood CapriSun and trail mix didn't make me sick anymore.

However, when I turned to him, he stared into the fridge with a frown.

"What's the matter?"

"There are no blood bags," he said slowly, and his words sounded more like a question than statement.

"Oh," I said, coming over and peering into the fridge stocked with everything except blood bags. Typically, The Order provided them. Crispin had explained what a nightmare it was to travel as a vampire. They couldn't take blood on airplanes, so they had to coordinate with The Order to pick up supplies at their destination.

"When was the last time you ate?" I asked and stared as he winced and rubbed the back of his neck.

"Well, I haven't in two days. Your parents came over, and then, well, I just assumed I'd have a couple of bags as soon as we got in," he explained.

"Oh, well...Will you be fine? What do we need to do?" I watched his jaw clenched and unclenched, his hands open and closed at his sides erratically.

"I don't know what to do. Call Jessica, I guess, but it could take her a day to get the blood here, and that means I could have to go through tomorrow without it." His breath was short, and he wasn't looking at me.

"Are you freaking out right now?' I asked, and I tried to hide the smiling lilt to my voice. I really did because I realized it's cruelty. "Are you freaking out right now while I remain calm?"

His head turned to me, and he served me a glare that freed my smile from where I had repressed it. "Maisie, this isn't funny."

"No, no, it's very serious." I composed myself, and he gave me an incredulous look as I pursued my smile into a line. "Okay, I'll call Jessica so you don't have to, and we go from there."

He went to sit on the bed, staring blankly at the wall as I recognized the helpless spiral of thoughts across his face. What a sort of horror all its own to be at the mercy of someone else to provide you the only thing keeping you from turning you into something you didn't want to be. I felt guilty for making fun of him, but it felt nice to be the problem solver once instead of the problem. I sat beside him, slipped my hand into his, and watched him visibly relax.

I dialed Jessica's number, which rang a few times before going to voicemail.

"Hey, Jessica, It's Maisie. We just checked into our room at The Henry, and there is no blood for Crispin, and he needs it. He hasn't eaten in a couple of days, and he thought there would be some here for him, so could you call us and let us know what we should do? Thanks, bye." I hung up the phone.

"Okay, so in the worst case, you don't get blood until tomorrow, and then what?" I asked him, rubbing my thumb over his. "What happens then."

"I can't go anywhere hungry like this, Mais." He exhaled. "Especially another day or even half a day. I'll be on edge, and if anything sets me off...." He stopped, and I thought he was imagining what would happen.

"Okay, how much blood would you need to hold off until tomorrow?"

"What do you suggest we do? Call room service and ask if they would deliver a pint of ice-cold human blood?" His eyes snapped to mine, irritation present.

"No, you'll drink some from me," I said, not an ounce of fear in me at that moment.

All the color drained from Crispin's face as his countenance fell. "Absolutely not."

"Why not?"

"Because I'm fucking hungry, Maisie, and I could hurt you."

"You could hurt someone else if you don't, and better now when you're a little hungry than when you are starving, right?"

"Jessica could call us back." His voice pleaded with me, and I then had the good sense to consider the danger of the situation. I knew he could hurt me, and maybe I was foolish to think he wouldn't. I thought that he cared about me enough that it wasn't a considerable risk.

"We can't get on a plane back home with you like this, and we have no blood here for you. We don't have a lot of options, and I don't mind."

"You should mind." He sighed, slipped his hand from mine, ran it through his hair, and rubbed his eyes.

"Let's wait until tomorrow morning. We can discuss it if we haven't heard from her by then."

"We'll wait an hour. It'll be less dangerous now than it will be tomorrow, right?" I pushed but kept my voice gentle.

He grumbled an agreement and then went to rifle through his bag. "I'm going to work out for a bit. It takes the edge off."

"Okay, I'll stay here and shower to wash the airplane germs off." I started going through my bag, hoping to detract from the nerves that were suddenly upon me.

I felt too warm thinking about Crispin's teeth sinking into my neck. Did I want him to bite me to help him or because I was curious? And why was I giddy at the idea, especially considering it was an emergency situation?

"I'll be back," Crispin called from the door, and I nearly jumped out of my skin as the automatic door lock sealed behind him.

My hands worked faster than my brain as I grabbed my toiletry bag and a sexy black satin pajama set I had ordered online. Crispin had said he liked me in black once, so I stepped out of my pink comfort zone for him. I had packed it, thinking Crispin and I might go further than just kissing. I did not bring them with the intent to wear them when my husband drank my blood.

I gripped the edge of the sink.

When my husband drank my blood.

What was wrong with me that I felt a warmth spread through my body at those words?

I showered and tried not to think about how hard I was trying to get ready for this event. I scrubbed down twice and shaved. Getting out, I moisturized and spritzed my perfume all over me before slipping the silky bottoms and lace top over my head. I picked up my mascara tube and stared at it momentarily before throwing it back in the bag and rolling my eyes at myself.

"You're being stupid." I chastised as I looked over the room service menu. I used their app to order the sushi that the restaurant below boasted was the best before I flopped down on the bed in disarray.

My phone rang on the nightstand, and I got up and leaned over to grab it and answer the call.

"Hey, Tru," I said, laying back down.

"Hey, girl, I just want to be sure we are still on for the twenty-eighth. Friend Christmas, yeah?"

Erik, Trudy, Briar, and Darcy would come for a little Christmas party after the vampire political mess. It was actually what I was looking forward to get me through the next couple of days.

"Yeah, I'm keeping my tree up and everything."

"I didn't really need to confirm this; I just wanted to talk to you," she admitted, and I laughed. "I miss you too and am excited to see you guys. I don't like that we are adulting now and aren't together all the time."

My eyes started to mist. Very few people could elicit my emotional vulnerability, but my best friend was definitely one of them. "Agreed, definitely not ideal."

"How is Crispin?" she asked.

"He's an ass."

"Well, yes." She laughed, "But that's your guy's way."

"How are you and Erik?"

"I found a ring box," Trudy whispered over the phone as if Erik was nearby.

I squealed with her as the door to our room opened and closed. I turned to see Crispin come in and head right into the bathroom. My heart was in my throat once more.

"Did you look inside?" I whispered because she had been whispering.

"No, I want to be sort of surprised."

We talked for another fifteen minutes, and thankfully, it helped relax my nerves a bit. When Crispin came out of the bathroom, I tipped my head back to look at him as he typed something on his phone.

"I gotta go, Tru. I'm starving, and our room service is about to arrive." I sat up after she said goodbye and plugged my phone into the charger.

"Did Jessica call back?"

I knew she hadn't, but I made a show of checking my messages anyway. "Nope."

"Ah." He sat on the edge of the bed, hunched over and dejected.

"How are you feeling?"

"The workout didn't help much," he admitted. "I just feel stupid for not eating before. I know better than to do this."

"Every other place we've been, it's been here for you." I placed my hand on his thigh, and he flinched a bit at the contact.

We sat there in silence for a bit. My heart was in my throat with anticipation and some nerves. A flush came over me when I remembered that Crispin would be able to tell.

"You gotta just do it, Crispin," I said finally after it was clear that he would sit there all night and stare at nothing.

"You have your hunter blade?" he asked, and I blanched a bit as he turned his head to look at me.

"I don't need it," I shook my head. "Also, how do you think I was going to get it on the airplane?"

His movements were jerky and abnormal as he stood up and paced.

"Alright, lay down on the bed." He shooed me with his hands but still didn't make eye contact.

"Where will you drink from? My neck?" I asked, instinctually reaching up to the column of my throat.

"If I wanted you to have a bruise there for a week, maybe." He scowled. "Lay down with your legs off the bed. I'll drink from your thigh."

"That's intimate." I was warm. The flush I couldn't control had taken over my whole face as I imagined his face pressed into the soft skin of my thigh.

He groaned and turned away from me. "Maisie, please, can you try not to be excited about this?"

"Sorry," I squeaked, lying down, and I covered my face with my hands. However, the more I tried to push the fluttering in my stomach away and the images of him kissing and nipping anywhere he wanted, the worse it got. When I lifted my head, he was staring at me with his hand plastered over his mouth, but I could see his eyes shift from blue to red.

Twenty-Three

Crispin

My wife. My fucking wife was going to be the death of me. She would be the death of herself if she wasn't careful. I removed my hand, hoping the double fangs present would deter her from thinking of this as something more than it was.

Because if she kept looking at me like that, I was going to lose it. *It's better not to look at her at all*. Focus on the spot I planned to drink from. Clinical. Think of it like a blood bag. If only the blood bag weren't attached to the woman I was in love with. Being a young adult was hard enough. Now, my nineteen-year-old vampire senses were overriding all my self-control.

I grabbed a hotel towel, wet a washcloth with warm water, and rung it out until it was damp. Maisie's fingers tapped against the duvet with nerves or impatience. I wasn't sure. I returned and moved her legs closed, stuffing the bath towel under her, trying not to touch more than I had to.

The blood was rushing in my ears, almost drowning out the small changes in Maisie's breathing— almost. I affirmed myself in my mind while controlling my breathing. This was necessary. We needed to do this. This was a controlled setting; the longer I waited, the worse it would get. It was better to do it now while I had some semblance of control. I was hungry but not hungry enough to hurt her. At least, I didn't think so. I had a lot of head knowledge of what it was like to drink fresh blood but no experience.

"Okay, I'm going to do this," I said.

"Are you sure you don't want to make the bed? Polish your shoes? Take another trip to the bathroom?" Maisie asked, and I shot her a look.

"I was talking to myself. Your comments aren't needed." I took a breath and dipped down, finding where I figured a vein would be on the outside of her thigh with my fingers. She had nothing to say now, and I tried not to feel smug about it. I put my mouth close to the spot I had picked, my heart racing. My whole body was flushed, but there was some excitement there as well—the very thing I had just chastised Maisie for.

"Maisie, if something goes wrong...."

"Oh, just do it!" she nearly shouted, and I leaned forward and bit into her as gently as I could. She fell back from where she had sat up to yell at me. A small surprised breath left her, but then she was silent. Or maybe I just couldn't hear her over the reaction my brain was having to her warm blood pooling into my mouth. I drank it down greedily, like a child with a treat. I heard myself whimper as my tongue worked over the wound to consume as much as I could. I was hungrier than I realized.

I would never drink cold blood again. Whoes idea were cold blood bags? Absolutely horrible. Maisie was warm, sweet, metallic, and perfect. It was so much better than they told me it would be. How could you even correctly explain it?

Maisie sort of sighed as I drew more blood from her. A surge of pride filled me, and I wanted to hear it again. I wanted to spend all day listening to that sound as I bit her, kissed her, and tangled my hands in her hair.

Then, there was a knock at the door, and a female voice declared, "Room Service."

I released her in a panic, reeling from the shock of my thoughts met with the reality of where I was.

"Damn sushi," Maisie muttered, and I turned to her where she lay still on the bed, her eyes closed.

"Just a minute," I called to them. I pressed the damp washcloth to the mess I had made on Maisie's outer leg, now smeared with blood. I pulled her hand down, showing her to keep the washcloth in place, and hurried to the bathroom to clean up as fast as possible before going to the door.

I let the woman in and apologized for the delay, as she apologized for the food taking so long. She looked at Maisie with disinterest, and I was overwhelmed with relief that no blood was visible the way she was lying.

"Planes make her tired." I tried to explain, but I ended up sounding awkward.

"Sure," the lady smiled at me before leaving with her cart. Once she was gone, I shut the door and sagged against it.

Holy Shit.

"Hey?" I called to Maisie, but there was no response. I got up in a panic, hurrying over to her and leaning over to see her face.

Her eyes found mine, and I exhaled in relief. "You scared me," I said.

She just continued to stare, so I got up on the bed and lay next to her, staring back. I reached down and laced my fingers in hers, and she squeezed them twice.

"Are you okay?" After a bit more silence, I asked, and she nodded but made no move to get up. "Do you need something?"

"Maybe my food," she said finally. At that moment, I was willing to give her whatever she wanted for the rest of my life.

Before I got her food, I finished cleaning up her leg. Grabbing a band-aid from a mini first aid kit, I knew she always packed in her suitcase. I cleaned the wound and put the bandage on, taking the towels from under her and setting them in the hotel laundry bin. I brought her one of the plates that were over an inset of ice; when I'd taken off the dome, I saw two rolls of sushi delicately decorated with edible flowers and ginger. I also brought her a glass of cold water from the pitcher. She sat up, still oddly quiet, making me nervous, so instead of enduring it, I grabbed my food and flipped on the TV. I channel surfed, trying to battle the mounting insecurity welling up inside of me.

I don't think Maisie hated me, but maybe she finally saw the danger. She had made the horrible mistake of tying her mess to my mess. I hadn't thought to wonder how much blood I'd drank. I felt better, satisfied, and no longer on edge, but maybe I had taken too much. It was hard to measure when drinking directly out of someone. Perhaps I had gone too far, and she....

She moved, scooted closer to me, and nestled into me with her sushi next to her as she watched me flick through channels. I sighed and relaxed, banishing the thought that I was unlovable—at least for that moment.

She was quiet the rest of the evening until it was time to sleep. We lay next to each other, sort of stiff and awkward. I kept opening my mouth and closing it, not sure what to ask her, not sure she wanted to be asked.

"I'm okay. You don't need to be weird," she said finally.

"I'm not being weird. I just don't know what to say."

"What do you want to say?" She sort of whispered it. "What would you say if you weren't worried about how it sounded?"

"What would you say if you weren't worried about how it sounded?" I countered, turning my head, curious at her choice of wording.

She didn't answer right away, so I let her work up the courage to say something.

"It was incredible, Crispin. Scary. I am so scared by how much I liked it." Her voice trembled a little bit.

My heart dropped as I turned my head to stare back up at the ceiling. I didn't want her to be scared; more than anything, I didn't want her to be afraid of me. I didn't want to make her life harder.

"It's just the reaction to the enzymes in my saliva, Mais. It isn't you. It would happen to anyone. Plus, it won't happen again, I promise."

I didn't like to promise that.

"Don't say that," she whispered, her voice not returning to normal. "That's not the part I'm talking about. I mean, yes, that part was mind-bending awesome. But after you stopped and you...." She faltered for words, and I imagined her face flushing. "When you took care of me and touched me so gently and patiently, you called out to me to make sure I was okay."

Then Maisie said the worst thing she could have possibly said.

"I think I love you." She began to cry.

I went to her immediately and pulled her to me, wrapping her in my arms. "Why the hell are you crying about that?" I asked, pulling her face back and wiping the tears from it.

"Because I don't know how to be good at it. I don't know how to love the right way. I mean, your family, your mom and your dad taught you how to love right, you know?"

I knew. I knew my parents had prepared Darcy and me to love well. They were both kind and caring people who made sure we knew what was important. Not without their flaws, but I understood what she meant. It was evident in the atmosphere of her parents' house versus mine. The Popes were more distant, almost clinical in the way they talked to her. And the Bookers, well, we were a lot, but...there was no lack of affection.

"It's alright," I said, patting her cute little sleeping bonnet.

"No, it isn't because I'll be so slow to learn how to be good at it," she sniffled.

"I've got time and a lot to learn too."

There was more silence, and I thought she had fallen asleep, but then she said, "You make me feel like I'm important and valuable, and I don't know that I have ever felt like that."

"I am sorry, but I should not be your first exposure to that, especially because I'm such an idiot."

"You are an idiot." The softness of her laugh had returned.

"You are my people, Maisie. No matter what happens now or in five years, whether we work out or not, you are important to me, and I love you."

"Like in a platonic way?" She pulled back to view my dimly lit face.

"Bold of you to assume we are friends." I kissed her nose.

"Friends with benefits?" she suggested.

"Married with benefits." I finalized, and she nodded, settling back into me.

Twenty-Four

Maisie

The Haymaks were some of the easiest people we had been hosted by. When we came over, they had a complete brunch spread and were super personable the whole time we ate. You wouldn't be able to tell that they were old money hunters as there wasn't an ounce of stuffiness to be found among them.

The grandparents, Jane and Lawrence, lived in a second house on the property and came in from their private tennis court during the meal. The grandfather slipped off his shoes in exchange for a solid pair of purple Crocs adorned with more Croc Charms than I thought could fit on a shoe.

They sat down and asked about our honeymoon and our Thanksgiving. The parents were Molly and Jake, and they had three kids: Jasper, who was in college and wouldn't be in town for the ball; Petal, a fourteen-year-old who had been reading quietly in her seat the whole time; and Weston, a precocious ten-year-old who was hounding us about our chess abilities.

"I play a little," I admitted, and his whole face lit up.

"Mom and Dad don't play with me. Can we play after breakfast?"

"Weston, these love birds might have somewhere to be after this," Molly chastised him as his previously happy face transformed into a polite pout.

"We can play a game," I assured him.

"You make it sound like your mother and I are cold and heartless." Jake pointed a syrup-covered fork at Weston. "We don't play with you because you kick all our butts, and you're a terrible winner."

"He does a winner's dance," Petal said from behind her book.

"Don't mention the dance." Grandma Jane groaned, and the whole table erupted with laughter.

The laughter of family, the banter and ease that came with it, was still astounding to me. However, Crispin looked like it was the world's most normal thing.

I still envied him for it.

"You two will not believe the ball the Novic's throw," Jane said to us, and purple Croc Lawrence nodded in agreement.

"Kitty and Charles are as old as us, and we've been going to this since we were... oh, how old were we, Jane?" Lawrence asked.

"Mid-twenties, I suppose, before Vampires were invited. Oh, no offense, Crispin, dear." The older woman colored slightly, but Crispin gave her a heart-melting crooked grin.

Well, maybe it only melted my heart.

"None taken, Mrs. Haymak. How long have vampires been invited?" He took another bite of a pancake coated in strawberry syrup.

He seemed content around people who weren't judging him for being what he was.

"Oh, it must have been about ten or fifteen years now. Since the treaty, it was tense for the first couple of times, but we mostly all want the same things," Lawrence answered. "Of course, there are radicals on both sides, but when you dig deep into the heart of the issues, we all want peace."

"Okay, Dad, that's enough morning mimosa for you," Jake said, rolling his eyes good-naturedly.

"Sorry, my boy." He took another long swig from the mimosa, mostly champagne with orange juice for color.

"I think you're right," Crispin agreed. "We do want the same things."

"The kid was a chess genius!" I argued as we approached the elevator.

"You got your ass kicked by a ten-year-old." Crispin played with the cuffs of his tuxedo after pressing the button.

Jessica had our clothing delivered. Crispin wore a black tux with coattails and gold accents. My dress was by Teuta Matoshi, in gold brocade. It had off-the-shoulder puff sleeves and gold beadwork detailing at the top. A four-inch black heel and some understated gold jewelry finished the ensemble, making me look like a shiny Christmas bauble.

"I didn't get my ass kicked. It was a very close game."

"I don't know much about chess, but I don't think it was."

I crossed my arms and walked into the arriving elevator.

"Did I tell you how beautiful you look?" he inquired, and I didn't want them to, but his words brought a flutter in my stomach.

"No, you were too busy mocking me."

"You're the prettiest chess loser I've ever seen."

"Insufferable," I said under my breath as he made his way over to me and leaned in, so one arm rested above my head as he drank me in. The appreciation in his eyes was too deliberate to miss. The desire I saw in his gaze matched my heartbeat and the want that pumped through me with every wild thump.

"Will you dance with me?" he asked, voice low and rough.

"If you act like a gentleman." I slipped my hand behind his neck to play with the soft curl of his perfectly done hair.

"I think you like it when I misbehave. Gives your rule follower heart a sort of thrill." He leaned in, but the elevator dinged and opened before his lips made contact.

He pulled back, sliding his hand into mine instead, and we stepped off the elevator together.

A hunter ball was much less dramatic than one would imagine. The floor was tiled in classic black and white checkers, the sconces on the wall and chandeliers were lit dimly, giving the room an enchanting glow. But the conversation was much as you would expect: finances, politics, and old friends who only saw each other once a year.

My parents had come, and my mom looked absolutely stunning in a floor-length sequin gown. My father was quiet as my mom came to see us. He stayed behind her with a glass of amber liquid, avoiding my gaze but managing to shoot a few dirty looks in Crispin's direction, who smiled at him without a care in the world. They went off to talk to their friends and we were greeted next by Jessica.

"Our babysitter in the flesh," Cripin said, giving the woman a friendly side hug, which I didn't think she appreciated in her terribly practical dress and heels. If she needed to kick your ass in her outfit, she could.

"How are you two getting on?" she asked. "I am sorry about the blood delivery; we are still trying to work out what happened."

"It's alright. I got what you sent this evening." He assured her, leaving out that he had drank a little more from me again before we went to the Haymaks, before the blood had been dropped off. I mulled over the memory of his mouth on my thigh, a little over from where his mark had been before, the purple bruise having blossomed like some sort of vampire flower mark. He hadn't taken a lot, and it hadn't been as traumatic as the first time.

I wasn't sure Jessica wanted to hear that.

In fact, I was sure she didn't.

"There's a professional photographer at these things, and he will be coming around to give you two special attention. But I wanted to say your social media presence has seen an uptick since we talked about it, and it seems less stiff."

"That almost sounded like a compliment," Crispin mused.

"Almost, Mr. Booker." She nearly smiled before nodding her goodbye to us both and walking off.

"What shall it be? Dancing or appetizers? They may not even card us at the bar." Crispin whispered to me conspiratorally, which made me feel like I belonged with him, like we were in on something together. I really liked feeling like that with him.

We ended up each getting a glass of champagne, and they did not card us. I didn't think the bartender cared, to be honest, as we sampled all the expensive food. We started playing a game that Crispin titled *rich people are bored of having money* where we tried to guess how much everything cost. Crispin was always way off, and I don't think I had laughed as much as I was in a long time. He came up with elaborate stories for old money vampires and hunters that swept the room and went as far as to imitate what they might sound like. When they turned to talk to someone, he imagined what they were saying. I was laughing so hard tears were in my eyes.

"Yes, Mrs. Chantilly, I just cannot believe they got caviar imported from California instead of the East Coast. You can taste such a difference, can't you?" his voice took on a British accent. "Why yes, Mr. Chantilly, I believe so." Now in a higher British accent.

"Crispin, Maisie." The authoritative voice came from behind us, suddenly silencing my husband.

His grandfather was there with his intimidating presence while also being dressed impeccably. He was a very handsome man. I knew his wife had died a few years ago, and my parents had talked a few times about how the widowed wives of high money circled him like sharks.

"Hello, Kirk," I said, saving Crispin from the awkward hello.

"You two look lovely." He nodded his approval at us, and I saw the way his eyes softened when he looked at Crispin. I wondered if Crispin could see it too. Maybe when he looked at him he saw his daughter. I wondered if he saw her killers when he looked at me.

"Are you enjoying yourselves? This is the party of the year, after all." He gestured around.

"We are surprisingly," Crispin said, finally giving the man a small but genuine smile.

"Well, I look forward to hosting you both tomorrow. Jaggar and Fern are coming as well; it should be nice to have you all together."

"We are looking forward to it, too."

"Yeah, I've been needing to talk to Jaggar. Is he here tonight?" Crispin asked, the edge of irritation tinging his previous good mood.

"No. he and Fern aren't attending tonight, I don't think, but they have assured me they will be there tomorrow," Kirk Hillbrand said, not picking up on any shift in Crispin's tone. "Well, you two continue to have a good evening, and I'll chat with you more tomorrow."

He stuck his hand out for Crispin to shake, which he did. I resisted the urge to cringe at the stiffness of the gesture.

We danced a bit after that, ate, and made our own fun in between greeting people that wanted to say hello.

"I wouldn't have believed it without seeing it with my own eyes," a woman said, as she laid an old weathered hand on my face in an uncomfortable act of intimacy. "But I can see the love in you both. Figured this was some sort of gimmick, a cheap trick The Order and The Guild were trying to shove down our gullets." She tsked as she walked away before Crispin and I burst into laughter.

We said hello to some people I had known since I was little. Then Crispin pulled me into a slow dance toward the end of the night, when a lot of people had more wine than they should have, and my lids were heavy from people-ing. I was near sleeping when our wedding song came on and as the band played, the familiar notes drifted over us.

"Did you do this?" I asked, pulling my head back.

"I did not. Maybe it was your parents," he suggested, pulling me closer.

I don't think my mom or dad would have done anything romantic like that for me, so I took it as the happy coincidence it was and let the music settle over me.

We excused ourselves after that, which took more than thirty minutes entirely too long, and I saw the same tiredness in Crispin's eyes as I felt in my bones. Too many people, too many words, and too many forced smiles weighed on a person's soul.

In the elevator we leaned against different walls and enjoyed the silence before it stopped before our floor to let a couple on who looked as if they were going to the pool.

"Well, Stan, look at these two, why you must have been at that fancy ball," the woman commented, and Crispin put on another pleasant smile.

"Yes, Ma'am, we were."

"Why, I bet there were women dressed to the nines and looking their absolute best." She beamed at him, and I felt more energy drain from me. How he could be so polite when he was capable of such sass baffled me.

"I'm sure there was but I didn't notice anyone but my wife." He smiled at her, and she replied with something southern and sugar-sweet.

I didn't hear the rest of the conversation. I was too busy staring at *my husband* in his tuxedo. With his perfect smile and lips that had just told this woman he didn't notice anyone but me in a ballroom full of people.

They got off the elevator and I was over to him before the doors had fully closed. He just smiled as if this was his plan all along and reached up to tug on one of my loose curls.

"You okay? That was a lot." His thumb brushed over my lips and down my throat so gently. It wiped out any other feeling. I was warm and content, and I needed him to not stop touching me. I needed him to not pull away at a kiss. I wanted to know how different this could be with the right person.

"You remember in Home Alone when that kid goes down to the basement and tells the furnace he's not afraid anymore?"

"Vaguely, White Christmas is my preferred holiday movie, followed very closely by Die Hard."

"Let's unpack that later." I pushed up on my top toes, and he leaned in a little, too, so our mouths were a breath apart. "I love you, and I'm not afraid anymore."

"You'll shoot your eye out, kid."

"Wrong Christmas movie, idiot."

His smile covered mine as he kissed me.

Twenty-Five

Crispin

She was on me before the door closed, pushing me back against it as I caught her. She pressed her mouth to mine in a desperate sort of way. She was begging me not to stop her with her fingers and mouth alone. I had no intention of stopping her.

I kissed her senseless. I reached down and cupped the back of her legs, hoisting her up to me. Trying to maneuver the dress out of the way, but it was a lot of freaking dress. Her teeth grazed my skin in a way that made me lose every rational thought in my brain. Her mouth found every sensitive spot I didn't know was there.

I sat her on the bed and leaned over her as she kissed down my neck. "I think maybe we should...."

"No," she said determinedly, and I laughed as she grabbed fistfuls of tux jacket, looking up at me rather annoyed.

"I was just going to say we should shut the blinds." I reached under her chin, tilting it so my mouth covered hers perfectly. Her breath hitched a bit when my tongue slipped along her bottom lip.

"That's all you better say." She pulled away, short of breath. Her cheeks tinged pink, and her eyes filled with a hunger that sent intense feelings through every part of me. "You've been putting this off for long enough."

"Are you sure?" I asked. She didn't have to tell me twice, but this wasn't normal. This was vampire-human stuff. I didn't feel hungry at all— well, not for her blood anyway. But it was still a little more risky than two young newlyweds up to shenanigans.

"I'm sure." She nodded. "Please."

"Such good manners." I booped her nose and got up to close the blinds.

"Maybe we should get undressed to get the whole naked thing out of the way." She wasn't looking at me, and her voice had taken the edge of nervousness.

"I mean, we've seen each other nearly naked. I'm unsure what kind of surprises could be hidden in our underwear. You got a garden gnome down there?" I looked down at her crotch to make a point as her eyes met mine.

"Maybe."

I took my jacket off and untucked my shirt from my pants. It took me a minute. These fancy clothes sucked at that moment.

"Wait, what are you doing?" she squeaked, but at least now she was looking at me.

"You said let's do the whole naked thing first. I can't very well do that with my clothes on." I stepped closer to her, sliding my pants off as her eyes tracked them. I stripped down, peeling my boxers off and standing before her to assess with very little shame. Locker rooms prepared you to be ogled and often worse. Maisie looked me over, and unexpectedly, I was a little shy and felt a blush over my face.

"Alright, that's enough. I feel like an art piece in a gallery."

"You think you're a work of art?" She stood up, giving me a sarcastic look, but my brain short-circuited a little when she unbuttoned her dress and shimmied out, revealing she wasn't wearing a bra. My mouth went dry as I admired her. I couldn't stop staring, my eyes finding her cute little freckles here and there, my eyes lingering on everything.

"Well, I might not be, but you...." I finally managed to stumble over the words in a way that was not super smooth.

Finally, after she removed her underwear and kicked her large dress out of the way, we stood there for a minute, looking at each other.

"Okay, I think that's a good amount of staring." I came forward, brushing the back of my hand along the soft place of her stomach. She retreated back to the bed, and I followed her, kissing up her leg and her stomach, then finally up to her mouth. I did feel anxious all of a sudden being able to touch her like this. Knowing I wasn't going to do everything right. She deserved everything to be right.

"I'm sort of nervous. Are you nervous?" she asked, pulling back for a minute.

"Kind of," I answered honestly. There was no reason to lie. "But we don't have to do anything more than this."

"Is that what you want?"

"What you want is just as important," I assured her, tracing the line of her collarbone and then between the valley of her breasts, making her shiver.

"I think. I'm not trying to, but I keep thinking about how it was with Ajay, with him over me, and I couldn't relax, you know?" She sighed as if she thought she was being ridiculous.

"I can imagine that would suck. Let's try this." I laid down next to her and motioned for her to get on top of me. She hesitated but eventually situated herself with her knees on either side of mine.

"Is this fine?" she tucked hair behind her ear, looking away from me again.

"It's great, don't worry about me." I put my hands in hers, tugging her down so she was over me. I gave her a quick kiss, trying not to go completely insane about the way her chest brushed over mine. "You're in charge, okay? Faster, slower, stop and go, you tell me. If you get overwhelmed or it's just not working, we'll stop."

"Okay," she nodded, looking right into my eyes. "Are you sure you're fine with me up here?"

"Don't ask dumb questions. Do you think I'm suffering?"

"Thanks, Crispin."

"My pleasure, Princess."

I don't think we would win the sex Olympics, but we both had a lot of fun. There were some awkward moments. Luckily, Maisie was on birth control, but we had to have that conversation mid-way. There was some laughing, some teasing, and a whole lot of good stuff.

One of the best parts was laying with her afterward and reading my family book club book on my phone, letting the contentment seep over me. Five years of this was going to be amazing. It was probably not going to be the easiest thing I had ever done, but it was absolutely worth it.

Falling in love with Maisie hadn't been on my bingo card, and initially, I thought I would have to endure her and these five years. But this was... different. This was better. I was happy, and I would do my damndest to make sure she was, too.

"What are the chances you want to order us some room service?" She mumbled sleepily into her pillow.

Twenty-Six

Maisie

Crispin's grandfather's house wasn't as elaborate as I had imagined. It was still large, with a massive driveway, but it seemed more historic than opulent. I found I liked that about him. And I was trying to find things to like about him. He didn't seem like an evil man, but Crispin had told me enough to leave a bad taste in my mouth.

When his mom and dad died, they had fought to take Crispin away from Nolan and Kat despite it being in Crispin's parents' will that they wanted him to go to the Bookers. Then, when his grandmother and grandfather had lost (despite all the money they had), they went no contact. They never tried to reach out to Crispin or have a relationship. That seemed very self-serving to me. To only want to have anything to do with someone if things went your way.

Though that was how my parents raised me, I probably only thought it was weird because I had been hanging out with Crispin.

We walked up to the door hand in hand. Crispin was in the cashmere sweater my parents had got him tucked in with some black jeans and a belt, and I was in a silky hot pink skirt and a cropped graphic tee Briar had gotten me for my birthday. It had an old cigarette ad with the phrase "cowboy killer." At first, I hated it, but it had worked its way into one of my favorite mix-and-match pieces.

Crispin rang the doorbell and squeezed my hand twice. I squeezed back.

“Good morning to you both, and Merry Christmas,” Kirk Hillbrand greeted us and ushered us inside. We passed through the entryway with a single wrap-around wooden staircase up to the second floor and a table with a glorious winter floral arrangement. He led us into a larger dining room with a sizable table that could easily host twenty people. The drapings and the wallpaper spoke of money, though not in such an obvious way as to be tacky, much like the outside of his home.

“I will give you the full tour after breakfast.” He motioned for us to sit down, and just as we were about to, Fern and Jaggar strolled in, chatting away, looking unbothered. The tingling of anxiousness started blooming in me as I noticed Crispin's posture shift. He was still planning on confronting Jaggar about the vampire club. I swallowed my unease, telling myself it would be fine. There was no need to get all worked up. We were just having breakfast.

“Crispin!' Jaggar said none the wiser to Crispin's souring mood.

“Maisie, come sit by me!” Fern waved me over, jumping up and down a little. I smiled, pushing the seat back that I was about to sit in and placing myself next to her.

"I love your shirt, very grunge princess," she whispered conspiratorially with me.

"Thank you. It's not my normal taste but a gift from a friend." She poured some ice water for herself and me, and I reached for it immediately to have something to do.

"How was the Christmas ball?" Jaggar sat on Fern's other side, addressing Crispin, who was on the other side of the table. Kirk sat at the head, took a whiskey glass, and drank a few sips. Whiskey and breakfast was an odd choice, but maybe old rich men always drank whiskey.

Crispin reached for the water pitcher before him and poured himself a glass. "It was everything that people said it would be. Very fancy and long." He took an extended drink from his water, holding his cousin's gaze.

I winced as Jaggar smiled and chuckled at his response.

"Leave it to you, cousin, to reduce the time spent at an opulent party to a few words, making it sound silly." He raised his glass of wine and toasted no one.

"They made a very handsome couple. Maisie, you looked exceptional," Kirk said, nodding to me.

"Oh, thank you." I smiled as two people came out of a side door and began setting beautiful plates of French toast and bacon in front of us. Fresh strawberries and little glazed pottery jars of syrup were also brought.

"My wife would have loved that dress you wore. Gold was her favorite color." He smiled down at the table, remembering something we couldn't see.

I was too awkward to know what to say, so I ended up just repeating my thank you and then looking into my plate with a frown, realizing my words didn't make any sense. When I looked up, I caught Crispin's gaze, and he was suppressing a smile aimed at me. I glared and shook my head, picking up my fork to spear one of the strawberries.

"Did you know that once vampires weren't allowed to attend that party?" Jaggar asked as we all started eating.

"Jaggar, that is hardly appropriate breakfast conversation," Kirk chastised.

"Why not? I mean, Crispin is married to a hunter. It's no secret that we haven't always been accepted in their circles."

"I did know that, actually," Crispin said in a clipped tone, and my worry started gnawing at my stomach again. "We visited the Haymaks, and they told us the addition of vampires is relatively new. And to be fair, hunters weren't accepted into our circles until recently."

"Because they were hunting us down and killing us," Jaggar pointed out while pointing his fork at Crispin.

"You mean while vampires killed humans without any regulation or control?" Crispin asked, but now he had stopped eating. I stopped eating, put a fork halfway to my mouth, and watched them.

"Boys, let's not do this at the table."

"Sorry," Crispin mumbled, stabbing a bit of his french toast and looking away from Jaggar.

"Noble Crispin, coming to the defense of people who have abused and smothered us for as long as we have been around."

Jaggar went on, and I looked to Kirk, who had a disbelieving look on his face, staring at his grandson.

"There certainly have been many mistakes made," I finally choked out, trying to de-escalate the situation.

"On both sides." Crispin agreed firmly.

"You're doing so much to make sure that this little charade of yours works, aren't you?" Jaggar's voice had gone from playful banter to something sinister, and now it was my turn to look at him in surprise.

"I don't know what you're talking about," Crispin said.

I closed my eyes and tried to manage my stress. If Jaggar kept pushing him like this, this could turn into something bad.

"No reason to play dumb; some people are smart enough to see exactly what is going on. A vampire and a hunter in love, how bold—how progressive." His voice grew more hysterical.

"Jaggar, you need to leave if you are going to insist on this behavior," Kirk said.

"I think I'll stay."

"Bro, we can talk after breakfast. Just sit down and chill." Crispin insisted, his eyes flicking between everyone.

"Here's the thing, little cousin, I'm here to make sure it doesn't work. That this heinous union that The Order and The Guild have put together just blows up in their face. If only because they think we are stupid enough to be fed their unity bullshit. And you defending them makes me sick. What kind of son would defend the kind that killed his own parents?"

I sucked in a breath and didn't need to look at Crispin to know how that slap in the face would affect him.

"Jaggar!" Kirk warned from the head of the table. "I invited Maisie and Crispin over for a nice breakfast on Christmas, and you are not going to ruin it."

"It's too late for that, I'm afraid," Jaggar responded.

I had long stopped attempting to look like I was eating. I gazed at Fern, who was looking at Jaggar with puppy-love eyes as if he had just hung the moon. The atmosphere of the table had shifted so terribly that everyone seemed frozen.

"I've put a nasty little drug into your glass, Crispin. Drops for vampire inhibition while making you a little slower, unable to fight back. Today is the day that this vampire and hunter coupling ruins itself in the faces of those who would try to shove their agenda down our throats. Vampires being forced to bend the knee to humans?" He got up, his chair making a terrible sound as it scooted back. "Fern Darling, will you go sit by my dear grandfather? Keep him in line."

Fern dutifully got up and bounded over to Kirk, who looked at her with his mouth slightly ajar. "Don't be difficult, Kirk, Dear. I don't want to hurt you, but I will." She patted his head like he was a puppy.

"This is not an amusing joke," Kirk growled. "Stop this immediately."

I watched Jaggar out of the corner of my eye as he came and stood behind me.

My cheeks flushed, and my heart rate increased. I could probably take either Fern or Jaggar, but not both, and not without my blades, which I did not have on me. They were faster and stronger than me despite my training. I looked down at Crispin's water glass, and his gaze followed mine.

His shoulders were stiff, and his eyes were angry as he assessed, weighed the situation, and decided what to do. But how much could he do? And what the hell had Jaggar put in his water?

"It's alright," Crispin said to me, nodding in assurance before glaring up at Jaggar, who had put his hands on my shoulders. "Jaggar, whatever you want from me, fine. Just leave Maisie out of it."

Jaggar's fingers tightened on me as he laughed.

Twenty-Seven

Crispin

"Aw, they're in love. How sweet." Jaggar's mocking voice grated against every part of me, which was difficult as I tried to remain calm. "What did you think? That the hunter and the vampire ride off into the sunset together? Live happily ever after? Grow the hell up." I saw his grip tighten on Maisie's shoulder, and my fangs slid out, poking into my lip.

"Jaggar, son, why don't you sit down?" My grandfather's voice was shaky. He was scared of my cousin, and I was uneasy as to the why.

"You don't have the balls for this old man. You wanted Fern and I to send her to that vampire club. You wanted her to get bitten there. You want this whole bullshit show to end, just like I do!" he roared across the dining room. Maisie was showing no emotion, sitting as still as a statue. I avoided her direct gaze, afraid I couldn't hold myself together if I saw panic or fear in her eyes.

"That was you?" I seethed, allowing my eyes to drift to my grandfather.

"That isn't this. Crispin, listen, I disagree with how The Order and The Guild are handling the new integration, and yes, I suggested if Maisie got bit at a club, they would pull the plug on whatever this is, but I would never put you in harm's way."

"Oh, shut up," Jaggar said, seeming bored of the conversation. "Our grandfather couldn't do it, so I will. I hope you don't mind, Pop. I put much more of the same in your drink, too, just in case you decided to get noble all of a sudden." My grandfather's eyes widened as he looked at his whiskey glass.

"You just had to ruin it by being in love with her." He droned on like he was the supervillain in an old cartoon. "Your pathetic little puppy eyes when she left the party, the way you went after her. But then I had an idea: I would just have to get you to bite her, which would be even better. If I could get you to bite her and then expose you for the horrible monster that you were. I mean, what kind of vampire can't control his urges and would bite his human hunter wife?" He leaned in and said closer to Maisie's face. "What hunter would let him? But we'll let you off the hook for that one, sweetheart. Maybe he pinned you down and forced you."

Maisie scoffed and turned to look at him with more hatred than I'd ever seen her muster. "He didn't force me to do anything."

"Such a gentleman." Fern cooed from where she was now perched on the table's edge by my grandfather.

"And the best part is, your absurd affection for each other will be The Guild and the Order's downfall. No blood is delivered to your room; all it takes is one bite, just a little, to tide over his hunger. Let's see if you did the work for me." Jaggar continued leaning into Maisie.

He pulled the hair off her neck and ran his finger down her skin. I met her eyes then, and her mouth twisted in disgust. Anger flared in me as I gritted my teeth to the point of pain. He inspected her throat for signs of a bite.

"Oh, such a clever one, my cousin." Jagger jerked Maisie's chair back, and the sound grated against the otherwise quiet room. He reached down for her hem. My grandfather was slumped back in his chair, watching in horror.

"If you lift her skirt, I'll beat the shit out of you and enjoy doing it." My voice was cold, and Jaggar smiled wickedly up to me.

"Oh, we love a protector," Fern praised again.

"You've taken your delights. Now I just have to tell everyone. Show them what you two are. You've painted the masterpiece for me; I must pull back the sheet in an epic reveal." Jaggar's sick laughter followed the melodramatic statement, and I began to loathe the very tone of his voice. Even worse, his speech and his looking down into her lap knowingly sparked shame in me that I couldn't escape. But I couldn't dwell on that; I had to save Maisie from this mess.

Whatever they had put into my drink started making me feel sluggish, as if I couldn't stand on my own. My mind reeled as I reached into my pocket for my phone and painstakingly hit some numbers. I hoped they were getting me to my speed dial. I wasn't about to look down in my lap to give myself away. I turned the volume all the way down and hit the dial before I didn't have the function to do it anymore. I slipped the phone into my pocket.

"Why don't you come on over here, Crispin? I'll need you for this part of it." I lifted my head to meet Jaggar's. "Up, lover boy. I can't have my saliva traces in her. That would defeat the whole purpose."

His hands were on her throat, and I pushed my chair back. It was all moving too slowly, like I was underwater. I labored over to them. Maisie was looking at me, but I couldn't focus on her.

"You're going to drink from her, right here, right now. A well-directed phone video sent to just the right people."

"They won't believe you." Maisie fought to be free of his hands, and I tried to get to them faster.

"Yes, unfortunately, they will. You know how hunters feel about our kind. The truth won't matter in the face of years of prejudice." He talks at her, patronizing. "Now, get over here before I lose my patience."

I wasn't in full control of myself. This drug could make me hungrier, less controlled, and less careful. I could kill her; this asshole would think it was the world's funniest joke. I reached them both after what felt like an eternity.

"You do it, or I open her neck up and...." He reached for me, and taken by surprise and unable to think clearly, he grabbed my wrist and bit into it. Blood came to the surface of my skin as I tried to jerk away, but I was slow, and my limbs felt hollow. I was also getting flashbacks of when I had threatened Morgan. This was some sick, twisted sort of karma. "We'll see how she fares against her twenty-three-to-one chance of infection. What terrible danger you've put her in."

"No." I gritted my teeth and yanked my hand back. Leaning heavily on the chair that Maisie sat in.

"Your choice." He shrugged and seemed unbothered, which made sense because a quick glance at my grandfather, whose head was lulled in a drug-induced sleep...or death, I wasn't sure. I couldn't bring myself to care much at that point. Fern stood by him from her guard dog position and gave me a small wave.

"It's alright," Maisie said low, and I knew she was talking to me. "It's alright, Crispin; just do it."

"I could hurt you."

"You won't."

"You don't know that." I pleaded with her. "Whatever he gave me...."

"Crispin, you gotta do it. I do not want to be a vampire," she said strictly. I didn't want her to be a vampire either, and I didn't want her to have to endure what that would mean.

"It seems you are only going to keep acting like a child, so I'll give you the toddler countdown," Jaggar patronized as I stepped behind Maisie. "Three, Two..."

"Please," Maisie begged, and I bent low, biting into her neck, hoping the person on the phone had answered. Hoping beyond hope she was listening.

Her blood wasn't as sweet as it had been. Whether it was from the drug or the stress of the situation, I didn't know, but as Maisie gripped the arms of the chair, there was no satisfaction in her reaction. There was only dread and self-awareness.

Don't puncture too deep, don't drink too long. How much have you drunk? Why won't he tell me to stop? How many minutes had passed? Had it been minutes?

Then Maisie slumped forward a bit, and I pulled back. "Maisie!"

"I'm alright." She managed, but it was strained.

"Aww, sorry, but you've stopped too early and lost the game, I'm afraid," Jaggar said, and I turned to find him, but he was already behind me. He used the surprise to his advantage, and Fern was instantly on my other side. She sunk her teeth into my opposite forearm. I tried to shake her off as Jaggar used my loss of focus to press my wound to Maisie's.

"No!" I pulled it back with all my stretch, knocking them both off me. My breathing was heavy and ragged. I stared at Maisie struggling to sit up, her hand reaching her neck.

"Don't, don't touch it." I walked forward and grabbed a napkin, wondering if wiping it would make it worse or better. I was frozen staring at her throat, now smeared with her blood and mine.

"Such tradgedies, man," Jaggar said from behind me, and I stilled. I wasn't as groggy as I had been before I drank from Maisie.

I turned to him, realizing without meaning that he had just fed me to the point of a blood high. Blood high was a state that happened when a vampire consumed beyond the amount of blood needed to sate their hunger. Beyond the threshold of necessity. And the blood I'd just consumed was fresh. Maisie was slumped in her chair now, eyes flickering open and closed.

I flew at him and pushed him further away from her. Using his hair as a handle, I smacked his head into a chair and watched as he staggered back, clutching his face. When he looked up, blood dripped down from his cheek where it had split. But he was smiling from ear to ear, like he had been looking forward to this.

Fern was behind me again, her long nails clawed for my face, and I shoved her back and to the ground. I'm sure she'd drawn blood as I felt the sting of the broken skin on my face. I reached up to touch my cheek, and sure enough, my fingers came back with some blood.

"You stay out of this," I growled at her, and to my surprise, she cowered a little from me.

While I wondered if I should pull back while I still had the opportunity and the competence, Jaggar flew at me, giving me no time to process.

"If I have to beat the shit out of you and claim I had to defend your pretty girlfriend from you, then so be it." He punched me in the face, and I heard the crunch of my nose as my temper flared into a fire I wasn't sure I could contain. "Might have to taste her myself, just to teach you a little lesson."

Fuck it.

He pinned my shoulders against the wall, and I met his eyes as I let go of trying to contain myself. No more suppressing the urge, no more being the good little Booker boy who could never live up to his little brother. He'd wanted to see an animal, so he was going to get one.

The blood in my veins told me I could do anything, and I let it assist me as I shoved him back and smiled through the blood on my face. "Teach me a lesson then."

He came at me with a renewed passion.

He hit me, but I didn't feel it. I'm sure he'd landed a few well-placed blows, but they felt like nothing in that moment. The blood gave me a thirsty sort of power I wouldn't try to contain. Fueled by rage and adrenaline, I came for him again. Then he was against the wall, blocking his face. The glimpses of his eyes that I caught were of overwhelming fear. Then he was on the ground, and I hit him again with open bloody knuckles that would no doubt bruise violet, but I didn't stop.

Didn't stop when he begged.

Didn't stop when he finally quit fighting back.

I hit him again.

His head flew to the left as I struck it, giving no resistance. Swollen, bleeding, and unrecognizable, I was over him, dropping my own blood into his once immaculate attire.

"Crispin! Crispin, please, you'll kill him." Fern keened from somewhere, but it was far away, and I couldn't stop now. This asshole wouldn't be given another chance to hurt my wife. He'd die before I'd let that happen, not again.

Then there was a hand on my shoulder, and I bared my teeth and whipped to whoever was trying to stop me.

Jessica.

"I'm here. I'm here, it's okay." Her voice was soft and kind, kinder than I deserved and more gentle than she had ever spoken to me before. "Let him go, Crispin."

I looked down, realizing I was holding Jaggar up slightly from the floor by his bloodied shirt.

"Crispin, we've got Maisie; she's going to be fine."

"Her blood, I—Jessica, I—" I couldn't finish the sentence.

"I know."

She didn't know. If I had turned Maisie into a vampire, she would never forgive me. Maybe, on some level, she would understand. Maybe she would realize I wasn't to blame, but I don't think she could ever forgive me.

I let go of Jaggar and found the wall slumping against it, sitting down as my emotions swirled around me. Tears came to my eyes, and I made no move to stop them as they fell down my face. My temples throbbed, and my lip was swollen and hot with a heartbeat. Jessica barked orders out at some medics who came and loaded Jaggar up on a stretcher.

I sat there, not even daring to look at the mess I'd made of him.

Maisie would be disappointed, my father, my mother, Darcy— what would they think of me now? And how was I going to learn to live my life without the woman I had just fallen in love with?

Eventually, Jessica came to sit next to me on the floor. My temporary tears had disappeared. And I was focusing only on the places I was in pain, fixating on the ache instead of my misery.

"We have to get you checked out too, kid. Maisie's in the mobile medic getting blood."

"What if she's infected?" I croaked out, my voice sounding like I hadn't used it in years.

"Let's deal with that later. Right now, let's have them make sure you're alright." She set her hand on my leg, and I nearly started crying all over again.

Twenty- Eight

Crispin

Maisie's parents had taken her to their house, and I couldn't bear to be in our house without her. So when I called my parents to pick me up from the airport the next day they didn't question me. I trudged into their house, beat up and exhausted, and climbed into my old bed. My mom didn't say anything. She had made me chicken noodle soup and warm tea.

Darcy sat next to me on my bed with his phone, not talking but just showing me memes and videos now and then. My dad came home from work and we all watched a movie in the living room every night for a few days.

A few days after the incident, I opened my phone staring at the texts she had sent me for the hundredth time, the swirl of emotions nearly drowning me. I felt like I had been holding my breath for a week, the place in my chest achy and heavy. Her dad had been right about me the entire time.

I'd lost control, I couldn't save her, and if anything happened to her— if she turned, it would be my blood that would have done it.

"Crispin, honey," my mom called from outside my door as I wiped my face.

"Come in."

Both my parents came in, and my dad looked a little more hesitant than my mom. They were dressed in their pajamas, and my mom's hair was up in her nighttime bun.

"Hey," I said halfheartedly as they sat down. I turned my phone over so I didn't have to look at her messages another minute. Messages I'd responded to a million times without sending any reply.

"Crispin, it's been five days since you came home," my mom started gently.

I waited for her to say more, but she didn't.

"Shouldn't you be with your wife?" my dad asked, finally saying what my mom wouldn't finish.

"She...." I choked out, my emotions strangling my voice. "Dad she could be...and I...I couldn't do anything to help."

I didn't want to cry again, but I was so close to it.

"No, Crispin, that isn't right," my dad said sternly, and my eyes met his, confusion filling me.

"The Guild called us and informed us what happened with Jaggar and your grandfather," my mom explained and some tension melted away from me as I sunk back into my bed. I should have been man enough to tell them, but I was so relieved I didn't have to.

"It was a bad situation, and you did what you could." My dad nodded.

"I lost control. I could have killed Jaggar; I don't even know how he is. Then I drank from Maisie. I fucked up so bad."

"All of that might be true. But you saved Maisie, and you called the right people," my mom assured.

"I'm so sorry. I tried to be like you, like Darcy—I just wanted to be like you. The harder I try, the more I'm just...."

"You're like you." My mom reached out and patted my knee.

"Listen, son, you aren't Darcy, and you aren't us. You've always been your own person. But we are so proud of you," my dad said, and now he was crying, so I started crying too.

"You're a little Booker and a little Hillbrand, but one hundred percent you. And your dad and I have never wished you weren't." My mom was apparently being the strong one right now as she forged ahead. "But Crispin Booker, why haven't you been to see Maisie?"

"I'm scared." I looked down and over to my phone. "What if I infected her, and she never wants to see me again?" I picked at the hem of my pants absently, not making eye contact with either of them.

"Well, you'll have to accept that, but do you want her to think you don't have her back?" Dad asked. "Don't you love her?"

I looked up then, wondering how he knew that. Had they both suspected before the wedding I had feelings? Was it my now sad and pathetic moping around?

"Yeah, I do," I confirmed.

"Well you better get yourself together and go make sure she knows that." He nodded.

"I will," I promised. As soon as Jessica told me if she was infected or not I would go see her, scared or not.

"That's my boy." Dad held out a fist for me to fist bump, and instead, I pulled them both in for an awkward bed hug.

Twenty-Nine

Maisie

Day 2 after incident

***Maisie**: Hey, you okay?*

Day 2

***Maisie:** Hellllloo? You can't even bother to show your face?*

Day 4

***Maisie**: You better be dead.*

Crispin didn't answer any of my texts. Two weeks had gone by since the incident at his grandfather's. My parents insisted on taking me back to their home, and I stayed in my old room, receiving daily visits from a traveling hunter nurse named Amelia. I hadn't lost enough blood for any permanent damage to be done, and I was just exhausted for two days. The real reason she kept coming back was to check my blood for the vampirism infection. She took a blood sample from me every day.

A week later, it was determined that my chances of becoming infected were meager. Amelia said she would check in a month. Still, the symptoms commonly presented themselves in the first couple of days, and the test was reasonably sensitive to any blooming vampire shift.

My anxiety was piqued as my thoughts swirled around what would happen if I were to turn. My parents would be devastated. Would they speak to me again? I knew what they said their beliefs on the matter were, but my father and even, on occasion, my mom talked about vampires like they were the worst part of society. What if their daughter became one?

Days went by, and I always held my breath as Amelia told me there was still no sign of it.

I had texted Crispin three times and called twice that first week. Unfortunately, I could see that he was reading then and choosing to ignore me. My anger boiled to the surface—anger that only that idiot Booker could get out of me. Didn't he even have the decency to ensure I was okay? Didn't he care enough to send me a quick text message?

When he got home, I asked Briar to show me a picture of Crispin. She hesitated, but eventually, she texted me a photo of him sitting next to Darcy with large bruises under his eyes and a cut on his face, looking like death warmed over. Jessica had told me that he had taken quite a beating from Jaggar and Fern after I had passed out, but they'd transported us in separate ambulances. I'd never gotten to make sure he was okay.

Something felt wrong about him not even bothering to reply to me though. I got angry instead of letting myself be wounded over it. Every day that went by as I moped around my parent's house, the more my anger festered into rage.

Even the visits from Trudy and Briar didn't help. Briar, surprisingly, did not make any jabs or salty, underhanded remarks, and Trudy did not dare to ask about Crispin. It was good to see them, but my mind kept going to how unfair this was. I was the one who was attacked. I was the one who was exposed to vampirism, and I was holed up in this house.

Even Jessica had called to check on me.

One day, I finally stormed to the front door and grabbed my keys.

"Where are you going, honey?" my mom asked from the couch where she was reading.

"To find Crispin." That was all I said, and I opened the door sourly.

"Maisie," my mother's voice had gone a pitch higher than normal, and as I stepped back to see what she wanted, she was halfway off the couch.

"Yeah?" I questioned, spinning the keys around on my finger, impatient to find and kill my husband.

"Crispin came to the house." She winced a little as she said it.

I felt dizzy with the change in my heart rate as I narrowed my eyes at her. "What do you mean?"

"Well, Maisie, you have to understand, Dear."

"Don't tell me what I have to understand. Just tell me what you mean by Crispin was here." I ground out now, knowing it was my dad I needed to hunt down.

"He came by about a week after you came home, asking to see you," she said, and I nearly growled at her for how slowly she was giving me the information.

"And?"

"And your father asked him to leave."

"Why?"

"Honey, what happened to you is that boy's fault. It was his family that put you in jeopardy."

"Jaggar isn't Crispin's family," Tears filled my eyes as my anger came out in the least helpful way.

They had no right to do this. This controlling bullshit they always pulled. Using me to get ahead in their social circles and then decide what was best for me when what they asked me to do all went south. Sending away the one person who I had wanted to see.

"Your father told him it was for the best if he didn't return, for your sake."

"Did..." I choked over the words, the tears spilling hot down my cheeks.

"What's going on here?" My father had come in at the wrong time, and I turned my full anger on him, slamming the door and tossing the keys on the entry table.

"Did you tell Crispin to leave? Insinuate what happened to me was his fault and not let him see me?" It was a full-on yell that came out of my throat, raw and unchecked.

"I suggest you watch how you talk to me, young lady."

"How dare you." I ground out viciously, wiping the tears on the back of my arm.

"Maybe you should go to your room until you calm down." He crossed his arms and looked at me like I was crazy.

"William," my mother quietly pleaded from the couch where she had sat back down.

"I raised you to be smart and strong, neither of which you are displaying now. You've become completely different after a few months with this boy. Use your head, Maisie. That vampire bit you, he took advantage of you, and then he put you at risk for infection. It would have ruined our lives had it taken!" His voice raised so that it matched my cadence.

"You're right. I'm not the same." I picked my keys up again. "And I'm glad to know that if something bad would have happened to me, it would have ruined *your* life."

"I bought your car; you'd better put those keys down. You aren't going anywhere."

I threw the keys at him, and he walked toward me, and I watched my mother wince out of the corner of her eye. "Keep it. Keep it all if that is what is important to you. I don't want anything you have to offer me anymore. For the past few months, Crispin has taken care of me. He's been the one who has dealt with all my anxiety and all the stress of this political game. Also, he's never treated me like a burden if I'm acting overwhelmed."

"Seems his bite has affected you after all," Dad retorted petulantly.

"William, stop." My mother was standing now. "Maisie, please sit down."

"No." A calm came over me after my dad spit out his last jab. I realized that nothing I was going to say was going to convince him that Crispin hadn't brainwashed me. There was no winning with him. No matter how much I argued, there was only what he thought and what everyone else thought. "I'm leaving."

"You can't," he said assuredly, as if just saying it made it true.

"Actually, I can. I have a house that The Order and The Guild pay for, so it isn't yours."

"What are you going to do? Walk?" He smiled, and so I smiled back.

"Yep."

I left my phone, wallet, and keys, only taking my ID. I changed into a pair of jeans Trudy had gotten me with pink daisies painted on them and the sweatshirt Crispin had got me for Christmas. I didn't take anything with me that was my father's. I picked up my room, leaving it clean and tidy, and sent one last text using the phone.

Maisie: *I'm walking to our house. Will you come get me?*

I walked around two miles before I saw Crispin's white truck turn a corner. The relief that flooded me almost made me sob again, and I came to a dead stop. He slowed as he got closer and flipped around a little after he passed me, coming up alongside where I stood.

He rolled down the passenger window, and we stared at each other in silence for a minute. I couldn't tell he'd been beaten up two weeks ago. His blond hair was shaggier than usual, and he looked tired, but other than that, vampire healing was incredible.

"I didn't know you came to see me," I said, shrugging, feeling ridiculous for talking so loudly over the running of his engine.

He just nodded.

"But you shouldn't have listened to my dad, and you should have texted me back," I accused, and he winced at the words.

"You're right. You stopped texting me after I came, I just assumed...."

"People with no brains shouldn't assume." I volleyed through the window.

"Pretty rude for someone who needs a ride. Where's your car?"

"I left it. I left all my stuff, well, my parents' stuff."

"Well, get in, Princess, we are blocking traffic."

We were not, in fact, blocking traffic. There were no cars to be seen on the street where I had been walking, but I didn't argue with him. I opened the door and crawled in, taking my place in the comfortable passenger seat and buckling in. I leaned back and closed my eyes.

"I'm sorry, Maisie," Crispin said, and I slid my eyes over to where he was. Head down, looking into his lap, his shoulders rigid. "I thought... well, I thought you'd hate me if you turned, and then Jessica told me you weren't infected, and I came to see you. Your dad told me you'd be better off if I just left you alone, that I'd put you in danger. That this whole marriage to promote peace was a stupid idea. Then I started thinking maybe he was right."

I slid my hand over and laced my fingers through his. He squeezed twice, and I squeezed back.

"I need you to take me to get some cigarettes," I said finally. "And you're going to have to pay for them because I don't have any money."

Thirty

Crispin

It was an odd feeling to be in city hall with annulment papers while The Flash Gordon theme played over the speakers.

Jessica had told us we were under no obligation to fulfill the five-year agreement, that The Order and The Guild would satisfy their end of our requests without us having to hold up ours. She gave us our potential schedule for the next year if we continued. She also gave us forms to fill out, made an appointment before a vampire judge, and informed them of our situation if we chose to get an annulment. So we sat in the faux leather chairs, waiting our turn while Maisie fiddled with her necklace.

Maisie and I had lived in the condo for the last few weeks. We ended up having a friend's Christmas a couple of weeks late, and the tree was so crispy that it dropped needles whenever someone breathed too close to it. It was fun, and we all played board games late into the night. It had been much needed, and I watched as Maisie's spark returned a bit.

I hadn't killed Jaggar, which was a plus, but I still felt a deep sense of remorse when I remembered what I had done to him. He was going to be punished by OOVA, and I would probably not see him for a very long time. Still, flashes of his bloodied face came to me at night. It had gotten less frequent, but the first week I had been back, I was pretty much a despondent mess. But when Maisie had texted me that day to come pick her up I'd never raced out of the house faster.

I hadn't stopped apologizing for two weeks. For not coming to get her sooner, for not telling her dad to fuck off, for everything. I think she was beginning to grow tired of it. Her words were; *If you apologize again, I'll vomit.*

She hadn't spoken to her dad, but she'd gotten coffee with her mom. That relationship was going to take some time to heal. I hadn't spoken to my grandfather either, though he had reached out via email. My parents, on the other hand, were as overly affectionate as ever. They showered Maisie with hugs and praise as soon as we returned, and she had only looked mildly uncomfortable.

After everything, we were getting exactly what we wanted—everything The Guild and The Order had promised without having to be married.

Is this what we both wanted?

Didn't we? We'd both filled out the paperwork.

"What does *so well as you* mean?" Maisie asked, and I looked at her where she sat twirling my mother's ring on her finger. "You never told me."

"*I do love nothing in the world so well as you. Isn't that strange?*" I quoted from the Shakespeare play I had read a thousand times since my mom had told me it used to be my parent's favorite. "From Much Ado About Nothing."

She let out a chuckle and a small smile that warmed me as we went back to our silence, until I decided I no longer wanted to endure it.

"You know what? We can come back when there isn't a huge line," I suggested. Maisie looked over at me, glancing around at the empty waiting room.

"What?" she questioned, eyebrows coming together.

"I mean, it just seems like a hassle today. Maybe we could come back tomorrow." I suggested looking at her pointedly. If we walked out of the court today, I would never be coming back—not for this, at least.

"Tomorrow, we have dinner with Tru and Erik," she reminded.

"Then the day after. Maybe next week?"

"Next week is bad for me."

"Next month?" I suggested, a small smile slipping onto her face that I could have kissed forever.

"I guess we can see, pencil it in for the spring sometime." She feigned mock thoughtfulness.

"I mean, we could do it today," I suggested.

"But the line." She leaned over the armrest of the chairs, and I met her halfway.

"The line is ridiculous," I agreed, and she kissed me before standing up and holding out her hand.

And so we went back home.

Epilogue

Maisie

Three Years Later

"Will you lace it up for me?" I asked Crispin, who was putting cufflinks into his dress shirt. He came over and tightened the back of the white corseted dress.

"You ready?"

"Please, like this is my first time." I snorted, and when he was done lacing me in, he kissed my neck.

We got ready around each other in the familiar way people do once they've been together for a long time. He handed me things before I asked for them. I tied his burgundy tie without him requesting it. He painted a fresh coat of nail polish on as I checked my phone for the time.

"I have to meet the girls at Briar's hotel room to get ready."

"Okay, see you out there." He came over and kissed me on the cheek. He must have thought better of it though and pulled me to him by my hips, kissing me properly.

"What are the chances we have time for some fun?" I asked against his mouth.

"Mrs. Booker, you are insatiable. Once already, this morning wasn't enough for you. You must only keep me around for my body."

"Well, it isn't for your sparkling intellect."

He scoffed before letting me head out the door laden with makeup tools and a curling wand.

"Do you, Darcy, take Briar to be your lawfully wedded wife?"

"I do." Crispin's brother's eyes were filled with tears, which I could see from where I stood behind Triana.

"And do you, Briar, take Darcy to be your lawfully wedded husband?"

"I guess," his salty counterpart shrugged a shoulder across from him, and he rolled his eyes before she amended. "I do."

I watched as they leaned in and shared their first kiss, and the small outside venue erupted in clapping. Arm in arm, they walked down the aisle. Briar in her signature floor-length black lace wedding dress and her groom as pleased as anything to be next to her. Darcy radiated happiness in a way that only Darcy could. Crispin took Triana by the elbow and walked down the aisle, then Erik and Trudy, who had gotten married last summer, and then Booker's cousin Edmund. It was a beautiful and small wedding where I could see the joy on all the wedding party, as well as the attendees.

The photographer instructed us this way and that before dismissing us to cocktails and appetizers while Briar and Darcy took their pictures together. I went to the bathroom to freshen up and then went to find my husband at the bar.

"Hey, handsome."

He turned, handing me a cocktail that the sign told me was *the* Briar.

"Careful lady, I have a wife, and she's kind of scary."

"Not as scary as the bride."

Crispin chuckled his agreement, sipping on his cocktail as we sat next to his parents, who were admiring the room's splendor. We all ate, drank, and chatted with each other. Complimenting the beauty of the ceremony and how much Briar and Darcy belonged together. They were going on a Honeymoon to Ireland for two weeks, and Kat kept saying she was so jealous.

"We'll have to take a girl's trip," I said to her, and she looked a little shocked at me. I had been trying hard to open up more to Crispin's parents. It came easier to me now, and I couldn't help but melt a little whenever Kat looked like she treasured my affection.

"I'd love that!" she gushed.

Finally, the room erupted in cheers as Briar and Darcy entered hand in hand. They kissed upon the crowd's insistence, and I leaned against Crispin.

"Ah yes, the fond memories of our wedding are all coming back," I said sarcastically.

"We've got plenty of fond memories to make up for it," Crispin pulled on one of my curls.

We have been doing our part for The Guild and OOVA for the past three years. I couldn't say if we were making any remarkable change, but it seemed as if tensions were lessening. However, it may have had more to do with time than a couple in their twenties attending parties and charity events. Crispin and I had become big advocates for Vampires and Hunters alike. Recently, Crispin even encouraged me to run for a seat on The Hunter's Guild.

"And plenty of time to make more," I agreed, standing up to congratulate my brother and new sister-in-law.

We drank, we ate, we danced, celebrated, and we all admired the way Darcy adored his bride. Those that really knew them saw the secret devotion in her eyes, sparkling back when she thought no one was looking.

Crispin motioned me over when I felt the night coming to a bittersweet end. I saw him snag one of the Polaroid cameras off the table and head over to Darcy and Briar. Her head was on his shoulder, her eyes closed, as her cold, dead, introverted heart was giving up. Wordlessly, we situated ourselves around them, and Crispin reached out with the camera. Just as he snapped the photo, I broke into a laugh as Briar's middle finger came into the frame.

Playlist

- **Too Marvelous For Words**
  Ella Fitzgerald
- **Bulletproof**
  FARR
- **Run From Me**
  Timber Timbre
- **How You Like Me Now**
  The Heavy
- **Jealous**
  Nick Jonas
- **There's No Way**
  Lauv, Julia Michaels
- **don't be sad**
  Tate McRae
- **No Angels**
  Bastille
- **Boyfriend (with Social House)**
  Ariana Grande, Social House
- **One More Night**
  Maroon 5
- **Deck The Halls**
  The Lumineers
- **White Winter Hymnal**
  Fleet Foxes
- **i'm yours**
  Isabel LaRosa
- **Catch Hell Blues**
  The White Stripes
- **I'll be Home for Christmas**
  Kacey Musgraves, Lana Del Rey
- **Till Forever Falls Apart**
  Ashe, FINNEAS

Authors Note

Firstly, thank you, reader, for taking the time to enter this low-stakes "cozy paranormal" adventure with me. Darcy and Crispin came to me after binging too many teenage rom-coms, and it was such a journey to follow through with their story.

Crispin and Maisie's story was a very emotional journey for me to go on. Each of them is deep, complex, and beautifully messy. Each of them is learning to grow, and subsequently I grew with them.

I consulted so many people who deal with anxiety on an everyday level to make sure to do Maisie justice and to best represent her struggles without making the story solely about her anxiety. Like Briar's type 1 diabetes, Maisie's anxiety is a part of who she is, but it isn't her whole identity.

I came to understand my friends and family better as they coached and talked with me about the realities and weight that anxiety takes on a person. It caused me to confront my assumptions and generalizations of what it is and what it is not.

I've come out on the other side of this story with a softer heart, and for that, I will always have these characters to thank. I hope this story helps people to feel seen and heard, or helps people grow into more compassion for something they may not fully understand.

Briar and Maisie are two polarized parts of my baby sister Willow. The salty girl who doesn't give one sh*t, and the anxiety-ridden people pleaser. These characters live inside my beautiful and talented sister, one of my favorite people of all time. And I think upon finishing this story, both of these people live a little bit inside of us.

Acknowledgements

I've already thanked my readers, but of course, I shall thank them again. I cannot fathom how I keep writing books, and people keep reading them. Thank you, always.

To the Lord for giving me the breath and the ability to sometimes string a sentence together. To my husband and my children, who support and love and allow me to wrap up in a blanket and disappear into my writer's cave.

Always to my beta and ARC readers, without you I cannot do what I do. Special thanks to B.A. McRae, Baby Willow, and Hayley B. for giving great inspiration and encouragement early on. Thanks to my editor, Riri, for making me look so much smarter than I actually am.

To the special ladies who took the time to educate me on anxiety. To those who have anxiety that read this early and gave notes and suggestions on how to make it better: Briah, Hayley, Willow, Becca, Emma, Stormie. You all have my undying love.

Hayley, you helped so much with this one, hugs and kisses, babe.

A special thanks to my baby sister, who takes heinously annoying phone calls about my writing and plot holes and scene problems.

That I get to write stories and put them out in the world is so unreal to me. I will never cease to be incredibly thankful.

About the Author

Author Monroe Wildrose has been stuck between the pages of books since the fifth grade when her father bought her a copy of Eragon by Christopher Paolini. When she's not reading or writing, she can almost always be found with a cup of coffee in her hand as she enjoys time with those she adores. She makes her home at the base of the Sierra Nevada Mountains, where she and the loves of her life, her husband and two rowdy toddlers, are fortunate enough to have Lake Tahoe at their fingertips.

Check out her other books!

www.ingramcontent.com/pod-product-compliance
Lightning Source LLC
Chambersburg PA
CBHW010423120726
47992CB00008B/3309